The Bleeding Mountains:
Clovel Sword Saga 4

BY GORDON BREWER

RAY IRISH OCCULT MYSTERY
A SHOT OF IRISH
(RAY IRISH SUPERNATURAL MYSTERY BOOK 1)
DIE IF YOU WANT PRAISE
(RAY IRISH SUPERNATURAL MYSTERY BOOK 2)
DRINK WITH THE DEVIL AT MIDNIGHT
(RAY IRISH SUPERNATURAL MYSTERY BOOK 3)
NO REMEDY AGAINST DEATH:
(RAY IRISH SUPERNATURAL MYSTERY BOOK 4)
DEATH STALKS THE RUNWAY: RAY IRISH MYSTERY CASE
FILE #1
REAPER WALKS THE GARDEN: RAY IRISH MYSTERY CASE
FILE #2

PARANORMAL AND FANTASY
BEOWULF: CURSE OF THE DREYGURS
INFINITE LOOP
THE CURSE OF BLACKBANE

CLOVEL SWORD CHRONICLES SERIES
SHIELD OF SKOOL (BOOK 1)
BATTLE FOR THREE REALMS (BOOK 2)
DOWNFALL OF THE GODS (BOOK 3)
CLOVEL SWORD CHRONICLES: OMNIBUS EDITION

CLOVEL SWORD SAGA SERIES
CLOVEL SWORD SAGA: VOLUMES 1 - 2
SKELETONS OF NILGAVA: CLOVEL SWORD SAGA 3
THE BLEEDING MOUNTAINS: A CLOVEL SWORD SAGA 4

The Bleeding Mountains:
A Clovel Sword Saga 4

GORDON BREWER

Brewer Internet Publishing, LLC
2023

Contents

Introduction

This dark fantasy adventure weaves another tale around the early life of Urith of Esterblud, also known as the Clovel Destroyer. Like most warriors of his lands, he remains convinced that his sole purpose is the quest for a glorious death in battle.

Following his betrayal by an old friend, Urith finds no relief from his self-imposed exile away from Esterblud. While Urith finds his fighting skills in great demand; each bloody encounter only brings the warrior more scars and pain. Even with his subconscious death wish, his luck and ability to keep the young man from finding atonement by dying in battle. Seeking to reach the Sky Realm, where his dead ancestors drink and fight for eternity, the troubled warrior finds the Fates have other plans for him.

Still traveling to the various trouble spots in Kamin, the warrior runs into bandits while heading to the small kingdom of Rarfell, which lies between Esterblud and Cahmais. When he arrives in the capital, Urith discovers a weak ruler and his queen who can barely hold the kingdom together. When the Gallaeci tribe takes over in an unexpected invasion, the Esterblud warrior helps the queen escape from the clutches of a ruthless warlord. Unexpected betrayal returns the queen to the capital, where the brutal nature of the Gallaeci rule turns the few remaining Rarfell leaders into exiles. Urith joins them in their escape, which leads to a showdown with his betrayer and the warlord.

In the encounter's aftermath, Urith must decide on a difficult path where honor and duty become tangled with his hunger for a woman who seeks retribution and his promise made to loyal friends.

The Bleeding Mountains

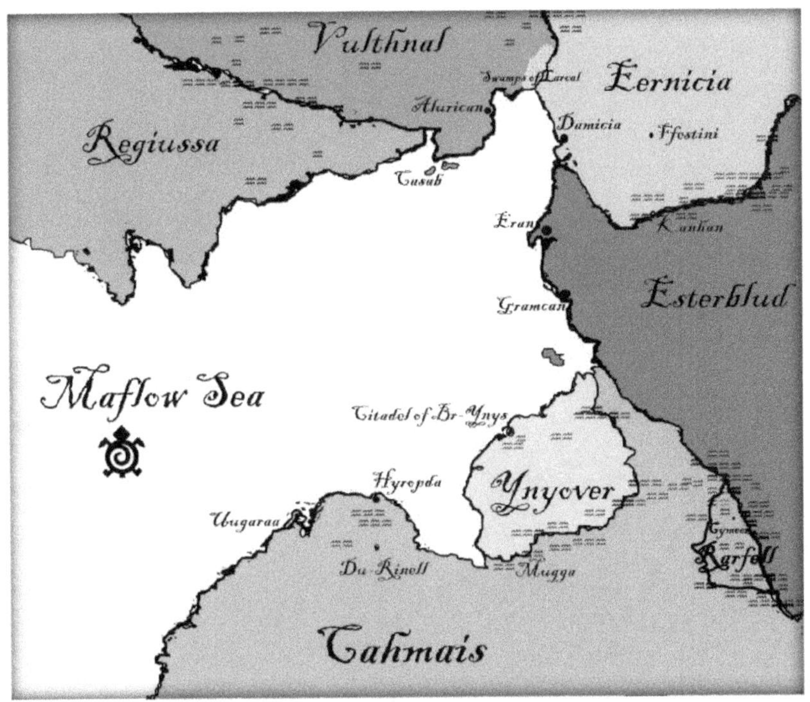

Chapter 1: Bandits and Fools

"Farmer, you've made a wise trade. Giving us your daughter, *ossane*, and *koinons* lets you live."

The hulking bandit jeered over the slight man in a brown robe on his knees. Recovering from his beating, the farmer could only gasp out another cry for help. The bandit's tattooed hand lightly tossed the bag of gold coins in the air in triumph. He pulled back the hood from his head to reveal the blue tattoos of monsters drawn across his lower face, which twisted like living serpents when he smiled. He turned away to watch his two laughing friends. They pulled a resisting girl toward their waiting ossanes. Like their leader, they wore black hooded capes over their tunics, and they had blue tattoos adorning their exposed skin.

Frustrated by the woman's continued resistance, one man struck the girl in the head with the pommel of his short sword. The girl collapsed. Instinctively, her father suddenly rose and rushed forward. The hulking bandit heard the man rise, and he quickly turned to step in front of the farmer. With a callous grin, the bandit plowed his short sword into the man's belly. The farmer's grunt of disbelief carried across the area. He grabbed his killer's brown tunic while he slowly slid to the ground. The thug watched with amusement as the girl's father opened his mouth. Blood poured out of the dying man's mouth. His daughter screamed at the sight.

"Well, that old man was a fool!" the bandit sneered as he turned back to face the woman.

However, the thug didn't hear the rushing sound made by the incoming spear until it was too late. Striking the bandit at an angle in the back, the iron barb spear tip easily pierced the leather armor. The mortally wounded man looked down in disbelief. A bloody spear tip extended from his ribcage. The thug fell sideways to the ground.

A large warrior wearing a black helmet rushed at the remaining bandits. Fueled by a raging fury, the Esterblud warrior growled with the ferocity of a cornered *batar*. The surprised men pushed their captive away and met their attacker's charge.

The battle cries of the men rose when Urith swung his long Clovel Sword at the first bandit. His weapon shattered the metal blade of his first opponent. Before the stunned bandit countered the stroke, the warrior struck him with his round shield. With a deft parry, Urith evaded the blow of the other opponent's hammer. The engraved blade of Urith's sword pierced the second thug's leather armor to embed in the stunned man's midsection. Urith savagely twisted his weapon, which cut deep into the screaming man's intestines. He slammed his shield into the man's face as he withdrew his sword. The Esterblud pulled away to confront the first bandit. The tattooed man suddenly threw down his broken sword and raised his arms in surrender. The only sound in the still air was the dying groans of a nearby bandit along with two fighter's heavy gasps. The entire fight took only a moment.

"I'll remove your head and leave you for the scavengers like your friends," Urith announced in his native Esterblud language.

"No, I want to watch him hang! I want him to die slowly as he gasps for air," the girl spoke with a bone-chilling bitterness. Urith glanced back to see her kneeling by her father's body.

"Have it your way," he huffed.

Urith pushed the bandit to the ground. He searched his prisoner and found a thin-blade dagger which he slid into his leather baldric belt. After tying the bandit's wrists with a length of thin leather. Urith picked up the thug's short sword. While he assessed the sword's markings, the girl carefully stepped closer as he rose. She stared at his green tunic, which covered most of the chain mail armor he wore.

"You are foreign to these lands and I'm not familiar with your shirt colors. However, I recognize the symbol on your helmet. You're an Esterblud. I come to thank you for your help," the woman explained.

The warrior pulled off his black helmet. He saw her reaction to his facial scar and he scowled. Her large brown eyes measured Urith, then she wiped away the tears with her sleeve.

Before Urith offered a reply, the woman handed him the bag of koinons.

"I offer this as payment for your service and to take this bandit to our overlord for his death. It is all I have, but I must bury my father."

Surprised, the Esterblud looked at the bag, then examined her. With a round, pleasant face, the woman dressed in a simple farmer's robe made from the wool of the highland *starkts*. A leather belt wrapped around her waist showed her curves. The top of her head came up to his shoulders, and she wore her brown hair in a bun. Urith tossed back the bag of coins to her.

"Keep it! You're a farmer's daughter. With your father gone, you will need it for your family. Besides, we captured the bandit's ossanes and weapons. We'll split the profit if you lead me to Cymeer."

Her face lit up with obvious surprise, and she quickly tied the bag to her belt. The woman watched as Urith went to his first victim and stripped the body of weapons. After determining his spear wouldn't easily come out of the corpse, Urith retrieved the dead man's personal items, then searched the other dead bandit. He looked up to see the girl trying to dig with her small knife in a patch of hard soil off the road.

"Don't bother digging a grave for your father," he told her. "Our prisoner has work to do."

The Esterblud pulled the thug up by the man's robe and untied his wrists. Urith put his sword blade on the prisoner's back. He threw over the prisoner's dagger next to the young woman.

"There's your shovel. You have until the sun reaches the top of the sky to dig a hole and bury her father properly. Fail this and I'll kill you slowly for the girl to watch," Urith coldly stated.

"Alright, you're the master for the moment," the thug declared with a bravado that surprised Urith.

He pushed his prisoner to the edge of the road. "Get to work," the warrior ordered.

As he watched the thug dig into the ground with the dagger, Urith glanced over at the girl while she went back to her father's body. He guessed she'd seen twenty *Gailcca* festivals, the annual event that most of Kamin celebrated. If true, it made her younger than him.

After the young woman removed several items from her father's body, including a leather necklace. She put the necklace around her neck as she walked to her ossane. The woman took the animal to the bandit's ossanes before she brought the animals over to Urith.

"I'll guide you to the town and stay to watch the hangings," she informed him. "Each week the king has these Borrs hung for their crimes."

Urith told her to tie off the ossanes to a nearby tree. His grin went unnoticed. The warrior liked her stoic resolve in the face of the violent death to her father. However, he noticed the bandit stopped working. There was a silent smirk on the man's face. Urith stepped closer to the thug and poked the man in the back with his sword.

"You need to finish soon," he warned him with a low growl. "I grow weary of watching you." The bandit sped up his digging while complaining that he needed a shovel. Urith ignored him as he went stepped back in the shade.

When the young woman returned to watch the digging, he felt the woman's glances at his scar that ran from his lip to his ear. While he remained self-conscious about the wound, Urith saw advantage in the dismay that his death sneer scar brought when confronting his enemy.

"I'm known as Urith," he said. "On my way here, I heard the kingdom of Rarfell needed help with these tattooed bandits. Villagers I met along the way called them Borrs."

"They're scum and deserve Caruun's torment." She spit at the thug. Urith pointed his sword when the man stopped working.

"You're running out of time," he warned him. With a glare, the bandit reluctantly continued.

"My name is Mekan," the woman replied. The warrior sensed her tension at standing so close to him.

"What do those symbols mean that you have on your green tunic with?" She finally asked.

"I'm a *Geniht*, personal guard to King Penhda of Esterblud. I follow the Code of Heptarc. That's why you do not need to worry about my intentions." He grinned at her. Her face remained stoic as she glanced over at her father's body.

"What's a warrior of the Esterbluds doing in the lands of Cymeer?" Her tone remained doubtful.

Urith leaned against a tree. He understood her concern. Their adjacent kingdoms used the same language, but generations of warfare between the various tribes of the area kept tensions high. His own king expressed once said that Rarfell was the thorn in his side.

"I got bored," Urith stated, following a deep sigh. Mekan noticed he looked away after the comment.

"Anyway, the skalds claimed your king needs the help. From what I've seen in my short ride, they're correct. They told me that your king pays for the live bandits. After looking at this scum, I don't know why he bothers."

Urith reflected to the last time he drank with the traveling bands of mostly male poets and singers who carried the latest news. For payment in drink and food, skalds retold the tales of elite warriors and their feats along with the history of the tribes and kingdoms.

"Neither do I," Mekan nodded in agreement. She went quiet, appearing to reflect upon his presence.

Urith left the woman and stepped over to one body. He ripped off a piece of cloth from one of the dead men's tunic. Urith remained kneeling several paces away from the thug who dug the grave. The Esterblud remained oblivious to the Borr who glanced over and hesitated. The bandit slowly went back to digging as the Esterblud rose and came back to the woman while he finished cleaning the blade of his sword with the cloth.

Mekan recognized that Urith intentionally stepped away. His gray eyes showed his disappointment that the prisoner refused to accept Urith's dare. The Esterblud's cold-blooded aim for the Borr to attempt escape surprised her. She glanced at their prisoner, who kept taking sidelong peeks at Urith. Mekan suddenly appreciated the callous waiting game, silently hoping the man would run.

"Mekan, where is your farm?" Urith's question brought the woman out of her thoughts. "Perhaps you should go back to the rest of your family? You can bring them to Cymeer for the man's execution."

"I have no family, only distant relations. My uncle lives in the hills on the way to Cahmais." She shook her head at the idea.

"Where is your farm?" The warrior threw down the blood covered rag.

"You passed it on this road. It sits near the fork of the river Ora." She nodded to the path ahead of them with a frown. "My father and I left the town this morning after selling our grain. We left the wagon with the blacksmith to work on the wheel. I was riding on the back of our ossane with him when this scum stopped us."

Urith took in the warm sun as he realized the festival celebrating *Ysbrydon* was nearly upon them. It was the time of year that brought growth and renewal. He recognized from the plants and birds that Ysbrydon came early to these lands. The warrior welcomed the warmth over the cold season of *Wyrnstrap*. He looked at the mountain peaks of Cy in the distance, which hid the fortress town of Kalh on the border with Esterblud. While Urith never reached the town, he recalled the stories of Gallaeci who controlled the area. The purple and yellow blooms of *the sawhorst* bushes appeared to cover the lower half of the range. Closer to them, he saw the blue fields of *vulgere*. The staple grain of Kamin fed both humans and animals.

"The bandits come through those mountain passes to raid our villages and farms." Mekan noticed the direction of Urith's gaze.

"They are probably going through the Ancient One's trail," the warrior observed. "The skalds mentioned the Gallaeci come here when the snow no longer falls. It's a strange thing to hear the Gallaeci moving this far from the mountains. We suffer raids on our villages from them occasionally, but they run away by the time our warriors arrive. That's why Penhda invaded along the border a few seasons back."

"Yes, and forced them this way! Even a farmer's daughter hears about the Esterbluds wiping out the villages of the Gallaeci." Mekan glared at him.

Urith glared at her.

"That's not true! I don't know who told you such things, but I led a band of scouts in that campaign. When we came upon those villages, someone already slaughtered the people. It was a mix of Esterblud and Gallaeci tribes who lived there. It was not Esterbluds who killed them."

Mekan remained quiet, but her expression told him she wasn't convinced.

Urith stopped the bandit from digging and pointed his sword in his face.

"Tell me, what do you know about the Gallaeci villages in Esterblud? Who killed the villagers?"

The man smiled callously. "Only the strong survive when followers of Phillo take a village. They sweep from the mountains like the winds of Wyrnstrap."

"You speak with a Gallaeci accent, but your dagger has an Eran blade on it. Are you one of these followers? Tell me the meaning of the tattoos of monsters and serpents on your skin."

The bandit's eyes narrowed when he spoke.

"Yes, I follow the redeemer of the Borrs and carry the marks of our clan. Our symbols come from Caruun himself. Each time we sacrifice to the underworld, our leader tells us which symbol to put on our skin. Phillo follows the will of Alrpan and Caruun to remake his conquered lands."

"Right, you can tell those worthless gods and this Phillo to kiss my hindquarters," Urith countered. "Now finish your work or I'll bury you alive to save the need to stretch your neck!"

Mekan gathered her ossane while the bandit carried her father's body to the grave. When the thug finished, Urith forced the prisoner to his belly and tied the man's hands. Then, the Esterblud went to a grove of trees where he left his black mount. As gathered the bandit's ossanes. He led the animals to the makeshift grave.

The warrior waited while Mekan made offerings to the gods for her father, using the grain from the brown ossane's feed bag. The creature placed its elongated, bulbous head next to the grieving woman as she spoke a prayer. To Urith, it appeared the animal mourned as well. When she finished, Mekan took the ossane's reins.

"Let's go. We want to reach the town before dark."

During their journey to the fortress town, the two riders kept a relentless pace, with their prisoner struggling to keep up. Urith had a long rope tied around the thug's neck. The prisoner jogged behind the line of animals, unable to avoid the animal's defecation. After his initial complaints caused Urith to speed up the pace, the prisoner remained quiet.

Mekan remained quiet as well. She said little until they got closer to Cymeer. Urith asked about the Rarfell and she told him more about her rulers.

"The people call him Renni the Weak," she sighed. "He's from the Rarfell tribe like me and many of the guards, while the queen comes from a once powerful clan called the Cyer. It's said that the overlord's frequent illnesses force Queen Darrca to run the kingdom with the help of her brother, Lerah. The guards are weak, and the fighters seldom leave the city unless they travel to villages."

"Well, that matches what I've been told. No one controls the countryside. That's probably why these Borrs are coming here," Urith glanced back at their prisoner. "I wonder why your army is so weak."

"I've heard men are deserting and going into the countryside to help their families." Mekan didn't sound convinced by her explanation. Urith asked why.

"All I know is the bandits take over roads more frequently. And there are Rarfell people who join with the bandits. Their faces carry the same tattoos."

Urith remained silent, his thoughts focused on warriors deserting their clans. It seemed too incredulous for him to believe it. He shook his head.

"That's nothing but a tale. It's like those who claim they see Fedelm or Wurms taking the spirits to Haligulf."

"Well, farmers missing from their lands is not a tale," she countered. "Soon, their lands will go fallow. Our people must drive out the bandits soon or famine will come during the cold of Wyrnstrap."

Urith looked at her. Mekan sat tall in her saddle, her eyes fixed on the road ahead. He liked her determination.

The trio reached Cymeer as the evening sun settled in the east. As they drew closer, Urith noticed Mekan kept glancing at him. When they rounded a bend in the road, the Esterblud caught sight of the capital of Rarfell. At the base of a white face cliff on a peninsula of a wide river, the town's thick walls of white sandstone hide the wood and stone buildings inside. The main gate stood open, overshadowed by the round barbican which held the guards. To Urith's mind, the capital of the Rarfell was underwhelming.

It's more like a village inside a small fort!

Mekan laughed at his expression.

"You were expecting more! I wondered what an Esterblud would think when he came here. I have listened to the stories of Esterblud cities since I was a child. The skalds were always talking about how the size and grandeur of the forts. They say the Citadel is even larger. I can't imagine what they're like."

Urith noticed how her eyes lit up at the discussion of his homeland and Ynyover.

"It appears you have wanderlust in your spirit," the warrior smiled. "That's something that I understand."

The woman noticed his expression change when he observed the guards in their blue and red tunics worn under leather armor breastplates. Their helmets of bronze were simple skull caps with little protection for the warrior's face and ears. Mostly, they carried spears.

How did this land keep invaders away for so long?

As the trio rode to the gate, a burly man wearing the tunic of the guards barred their way. He eyed Urith suspiciously, but his proper attention focused on the girl who rode beside the Esterblud.

"Mekan, what are you doing back here?"

She told him about her father and her encounter with the thugs. The man's face turned sympathetic as he listened. He patted her leg.

"I'm truly sorry for your loss. We'll string him up in the morning," the leader of the guards waved for the nearby men to join him.

"Your father was a good man. You should wait in town for your uncle. I can send word to him. Let's go to the *mear* with this information. He's with the elders at home. That's the third time today I've heard of these bandits."

"Thank you, Hera," Mekan replied quietly. "Those Borrs had me until this Esterblud killed them. This is the only one who surrendered."

Urith unhooked his rope and handed the prisoner over to Hera. As the men removed the bandit, he cursed them.

"Phillo will soon arrive to smash your heads," the bound man yelled while he struggled. The guards pummeled him. He fell quiet, and they dragged the bandit through the gate.

"Esterblud, you go with us," Hera spoke to Urith. His order caused the big warrior to sneer.

"I planned on it."

He spurred his mount forward with the extra ossanes, then waited at the gate as Mekan finished her conversation with Hera. The guard led her ossane to Urith before getting on one mount. Together, they entered the town.

Urith looked over the buildings made of heavy timber frames with wall made of a plaster mix of clay and straw. It reminded him a bit of his home village. They pulled in front of the mear's home, a squat building made of the same white stone. After the visitors slid off their mounts and tied their ossanes to posts, Hera led them inside. The group entered a room where a balding man in a purple robe stood. The mear sat huddled in conversation with a group of elders around a small table.

While Urith and Mekan waited, Hera went to the man in purple and spoke to him briefly. They saw the man look over with interest, his blue eyes carefully assessing Urith.

Hera came back with the news. He wasn't happy.

"Come with me. Rech wishes to speak with you alone when he's finished with the elders." The guard led them into the hall, and they stopped in an alcove by the main staircase. There were guards with silver-colored helmets holding halberds at the bottom of the stairs. Before long, Rech joined the group.

"You have my sympathy, Mekan. I knew your father since your farm is near the home of my ancestors," he told her. "I'll ensure that he's avenged."

Mekan pursed her thin lips, visibly holding in her grief, and thanked Rech.

"This Esterblud warrior interceded upon my family's behalf." Her tone grew hard. "The situation on the main road is terrible. My father would still be alive if the Rarfell warriors left this town and guarded the main roads."

Rech glared, but his expression soon softened.

"Unfortunately, you may be correct," he admitted with a sigh. "You don't realize the threats against the overlord which require our forces to remain inside the walls. We have rumors of assassins. I must keep the king upstairs in order to work. This is the reason we're putting together the Cymeer Company to help with our security."

The man looked over at Urith.

"You're a young man, but I see you carry the colors of King Penhda. You know that our agreement with your king keeps warriors from crossing our lands."

"I'm here on my accord. Penhda knows nothing of my recent travels," Urith stated bluntly. "I leave the politics to overlords and their advisors." His gray eyes showed Rech that he didn't like the direction of the conversation.

"Yes, I see. Well, you are certainly well-equipped for a mercenary," Rech crossed his arms as he glanced at Hera.

"If you come to join our company, I must tell you we are not a rich kingdom. We intend to add volunteers were possible. Most of your pay comes food and supplies for you and your ossane. There is a bounty of a few koinons for live prisoners and nothing for the dead ones. Any additional funds you receive comes from their captured weapons and mounts. We want those with a thirst for adventure and battle."

"We've decided to pool the spoils of battle, then split them among the fighters," Hera interceded. "The company seeks a group of warriors who follow our king's orders. We're not looking for rogues who seek their own glory."

"In my travel, I've heard the kingdom of Rarfell seeks honorable warriors." Urith growled out. "I'm Urith, known in my lands as the Clovel Destroyer. I don't seek your koinons, only to fight and die in battle. My spirit longs for Haligulf, to drink with my ancestors. If your men will not ride out against bandits, then keep them inside your walls with the women. Then, let warriors put down such rabble."

Hera moved at Urith, his hand going to his weapon. Rech stopped him with a hand on the guard's shoulder.

"No, I know about this warrior. I met his brother, Pehnuwick once. Their family carries ambition." He turned back to Urith. "I recognize your name and the sword. You're one of the few to kill the Clovel monster."

Urith nodded. "The pommel end of my sword carries the bone ash of the creature that I destroyed. Am I worthy of your fight?"

Rech glanced at Hera, then smiled.

"Urith, the skalds have a song about your fights in Esterblud. We carry no ill will about your intentions; however, we have men who travel into our lands only to disappear when they learn our terms. We're concerned they travel to our enemy and join them."

The man stepped closer to Urith as his expression turned somber.

"However, I take issue with your slight against the Rarfell warriors. Their noble men who fight against an unseen enemy. What you claim is a disservice to King Renni and his men. Your land holds many fighters along with a vast treasury. King Penhda and your brother know of our plight. I'd hope you sought their counsel before you left your kingdom."

The Esterblud took a deep breath.

"You have my apology, Rech. What you say is true. Before I left my home, my king mentioned he considers you to be a wise and honorable man. Pehnuwick told me of the pressures your king faces from Ynyover and Esterblud." He nodded to Hera with a guilty frown.

"One day, I'll learn not to let my quick temper overcome my manners."

He watched Hera back away, but the guard's expression remained skeptical. However, the tension dissipated when Rech took Urith by the arm.

"That is well said, my young fighter. You've shown us the humility of a noble person. Come, let's not dwell on such things. Warriors are notorious for their temper. It's a good thing for battle, but it makes diplomacy difficult, does it not?"

Rech led the warrior down the hallway to the entrance.

"I'm honored that you wish to join us. I'm afraid that our Cymeer Company needs more men with your ambition to fight. However, the good news is you will not need to wait long to help us drive out the Borrs. I just received more information that the bandits are massing along the border. We will send you and the others who join the cause to Eleb. You will follow a small detachment of Rarfell guards who will lead you."

"Do you have many volunteers?" Urith glanced over at Mekan, who remained close.

"Unfortunately, only a handful of men with your capabilities joined our cause. However, there is no need for concern. The enemy is not strong and they lack the fighting spirit. It's amusing in a way. Their leader is a fanatic who claims he's a demi-god." Rech let out a mocking laugh, and Hera smiled.

"Take your ossane to the stable and tell them that I sent you. The nearby tavern will provide you a place to stay. We'll meet tomorrow after the morning hangings. If you accept our terms, you will receive your instructions and meet the rest who join the Cymeer Company."

"I accept your gracious offer," Urith glanced over at Mekan, who remained quiet. "I'll return tomorrow."

When they reached the entrance, Mekan followed Urith outside. She got on her ossane and he asked her destination.

"I'm staying with you," she informed him.

"Don't you have relatives or friends here that you can stay with?"

"No, and you don't know the town. I can guide us to the ossane trader," she spurred her mount and hurried away. Shaking his head, Urith followed her.

They left their ossanes at the stable, where Mekan and Urith split the koinon they made on the bandit's ossanes. After throwing his bedroll and a leather bag over one shoulder, he followed Mekan to the tavern on the corner before the principal route out of the village. Its small sign showed the picture of a cask and the skull of an ossane.

Turning the corner of the plaster and wood building, Urith barely noticed a young boy who leaned against the wall. When he felt a slight tug on his waist belt, the warrior's reflexes were too fast for the boy. Urith grabbed the thief's arm just as he tried to pull away. The warrior's small leather bag of koinons fell on the street.

"Stop it," the boy complained.

"Pick it up," Urith told him. He gave the frail arm a twist for emphasis.

"Alright, alright." The boy picked up the bag and gave it to Urith.

"I like to cut a thief's fingers off," the warrior lied as he handed the bag to Mekan, who watched them. The boy's blue eyes widened at the threat.

"What's your name?"

"Dutra is my name. Now let me go. You're hurting my arm."

"Alright but don't you move," Urith warned as he let go. Dutra looked around for a means to escape while he shook his arm. The appearance of starvation covered his thin, unwashed body. He wore ripped pieces of rags as clothes. The boy's nervous manner reminded Urith of a *feorag*, little nut eating creatures of the forest.

"You got family?" Mekan asked. Dutra shook his head, sending his long dirty brown hair into his face.

"Alright, go to the ossane trader. I want our ossanes brushed. Tell the trader that the Esterblud sent you to do this job. You do it well and you'll earn a koinon and a meal." Urith explained.

Dutra hesitated.

"What are you waiting for?" He asked.

"Be careful in there," the boy warned. Then he turned and hurried away.

Urith felt Mekan staring at him.

"You're a strange one," the woman handed back the bag of koinons.

The warrior nodded. "Some will say that. But I need someone who knows this place. I've found that a youth will notice many things adults overlook. Besides, it beats breaking his arm for the information." He started for the front door to the tavern.

"I'm going to the temple and give prayers for my father." Mekan informed him. Before Urith could reply, she was already going into the hard-packed street.

As he watched the woman swiftly dodge the few ossanes and a wagon passing by, the warrior remained intrigued. Mekan held up well after her terrible experience earlier that day. He held no doubt that the woman suffered from pain and loss before. It made her resilient.

Urith entered the building through the open door. He noticed two men sitting at the end of a long table. The warrior immediately guessed they were local thugs when he observed their weapons and lack of metal armor. They kept staring even when he cast them a cursory glance. Urith turned his attention to a one-eyed man in a dirty brown robe who stood behind the thick wood bar. Two casks sat on the dirty floor beneath the man. He had his boot resting on the edge of one barrel. Behind him on one small shelf sat clay mugs and another cask.

"I'm looking for a room," Urith told him as he shrugged off the bag and bedroll on his shoulder. "Rech told me you would have one."

"An Esterblud, eh? We don't get many of your kind here," a gruff voice spoke from behind Urith.

Urith kept his focus on the tavern owner. The man's one good eye widened as the men from the back of the room approached.

"I said a room," Urith repeated to the tavern owner.

"The tavern doesn't take your kind," the voice behind him said. "How much do you want for that girl we saw outside?"

With a sigh, Urith pulled off two spears and slid them onto the wooden top of the bar. Then, he sat down his black helmet with his weapons. The Esterblud helmet had rounded slits for the eyes, giving the impression of an executioner's mask. He left his shield hanging over his back.

In a flash, he whipped out his Clovel Sword as he spun around to face the men. One thug held his short sword in his hand while the large man next to him kept his heavy mace remained attached to his waist belt. Both had leather breastplates, which were as scarred as their faces and arms. Their brown robes were cheap and tattered with wear.

"You couldn't pay an alley *docke* enough to sleep with you," Urith growled. "

"Yartha, don't make trouble with my customers. We have room for the Esterblud," the owner of the tavern tried to intercede.

"Shut up," the large man growled out. "I'm waiting for the youngster to wet his breeches. Then he can hand me his weapons and we won't hurt him."

Urith's eyes narrowed as the men stood there while the few remaining customers scrambled away from the coming fight.

"Pull your weapon or do you let your little man fight for you, *calward*?" Urith gave his death sneer.

The large man laughed. "You don't scare easily. Are you dumb enough to die for your weapons?"

"Yes, because the glory of Haligulf awaits me. The only thing that waits for you is the ditch where you rot with the trash!"

Yartha scowled, visibly flustered by Urith's refusal to back down. The man glanced at his companion, then nodded. "Perhaps you're correct, but we can't stop now." He pulled his heavy mace. "Selling that longsword and your chain mail brings me enough for my risk."

"Then, I guess you will die," Urith agreed.

The clash of swords immediately rang out as the two men attacked Urith. The fury of the blows pushed the Esterblud back. He countered, getting close enough to slam his fist into the ruffian's nose. Urith couldn't follow up as he sensed a blow coming. He lifted his shoulder in time to ward off a sword blade coming at him from the other side. With practice precision, Urith pulled his *Sgian* dagger while he spun around. He jammed the blade into the man's eye. The smaller thug's death cry stopped before he hit the floor.

Urith heard someone yell out a warning, but he immediately felt the blow of heavy iron strike his back. It missed his shield and landed high near his shoulder blade. The force of the blow spun the Esterblud around and he fell into the rough wood table. His large opponent continued swinging his mace, striking Urith in the arm with a glancing blow. The Esterblud kicked out with his boot and caught the charging mercenary in the groin. With a surprised grunt, Yartha backed away as Urith slid to the dirty floor. He groaned from the pain in his shoulder. His arm was nearly numb. His Clovel Sword fell out of his numb hand when he tried to rise.

"*Pitshog*, you'll pay," Yartha bellowed.

The large thug rushed again and lifted the large iron weapon to bring down on Urith, who awkwardly rolled away. The spinning move placed Urith under the table. He kicked with both feet into the bench, sending it into the ruffian's knees. Urith's opponent tumbled over the wood. The Esterblud struck out with his dagger and caught the man in the arm. The two fighters rolled away and got to their feet on the other side of the table. After he quickly surveyed his bleeding arm, Yartha reassessed his opponent.

"Your sword is behind me, Esterblud. That dagger won't stop me."

"Your betting your life on it," Urith sneered with false confidence. He hoped the man couldn't tell his right arm remained numb.

The ruffian came at the Esterblud. As he stepped around the table, the man suddenly yelled out and dropped to the floor. Behind him, Mekan held one of Urith's spears. The tip showed red with blood.

As Urith struggled to his feet, several Rarfell guards entered the tavern with their weapons drawn. Hera, along with the one-eyed tavern owner, pushed through the men in blue and red tunics.

"Back away now," Hera ordered.

Urith glanced over, then slowly backed away. He went around the table and picked up his Clovel Sword. The mercenary on the floor held the back of his thigh, cursing loudly.

"You'll go before Renni, then spend your time in a cell," Hera went to Urith. "Hand me your sword."

"You don't take a sword from an Esterblud," the warrior growled as he painfully lifted the weapon with his injured arm.

Mekan stepped between the two men. She still held Urith's spear.

"Do you plan on putting me in the dungeon as well? I fought with the Esterblud."

Hera's surprised look caused the ruffian to give an unpleasant laugh. Yartha struggled to sit on the bench next to the woman.

"You can't stand us in front of King Renni. This was a fight among friends." The ruffian groaned out.

Hera glared at the man. "Yartha, you've hung around this tavern, causing us problems for too long. You can't get out of this killing. The king will take your weapons and banish you. You can starve on the roads in the mountains."

"No, he won't bother with me or the others," Yartha suddenly grinned. "There was no killing."

"Then how did the man at your feet die?"

"It was an accident," the wounded man stated confidently. He nodded at Mekan for the piece of cloth rag that she handed him.

"What do you mean, an accident?" Hera went over to the body of Yartha's friend. "A dagger killed him from the wound that I see." The Rarfell leader looked over at Urith, who wiped the drying blood off from his weapon using his leather breeches.

"We were playing a game. The Esterblud threw his dagger into the ceiling and it came down, striking my friend in the eye. The Fates were against him."

Urith, like those around Yartha, stared in disbelief at the obvious lie. However, the guards standing around broke out in laughter.

"The Fates are fickle," Yartha shook his head as he finished tying the cloth around his wound.

"Doesn't the Renni have more important things to worry about, like removing the Borrs from our lands?" Mekan handed Hera the spear she held. "These men are done with their game."

Hera looked at the spear, then glanced at the two men and the woman. He sighed before an idea brought an evil grin to his face.

"Alright, no one goes before our overlord. But I have one condition," he stared at the ruffian. "Yartha, you've just volunteered to join the Renni's volunteers on their quest to remove the Borr's from our land." Hera smiled when Yartha glared at him. "Otherwise, the king will hear your crazy story."

"He won't laugh!" Hera stuck Urith's spear into the floor next to Yartha.

"Be at the execution tomorrow. Rech and I will explain your duties. If you're not there, the guards will come for you." The leader of the Rarfell guards scowled at Mekan before walking back through his men.

Slowly, the crowd dispersed. The tavern keeper directed two men to haul away the body of Yartha's partner. As they worked, he went to Urith.

"I've got a place upstairs for you. It'll be a koinon." The man smiled warily.

Urith nodded as he pulled himself up and went to the bar.

"Then, give me a heathmead."

Suppressing a groan, he slid his long sword into his leather sheath. Yartha hobbled over to the bar.

"I'll give you credit, Esterblud, you're a tough one." The man ordered a barkmead, a cheap drink that Urith avoided. "It's too bad you have a soft spot for that cursed code you warrior's always abuse people with."

Urith glanced over, but Yartha showed him no ill will with his statement.

"There are those who misuse the Heptarc Code. You'd make a fair warrior if you followed it," the Esterblud replied grudgingly as he tipped back his clay mug. "It might keep you from hanging at the pleasure of a king."

Yartha cackled at the jest, then lightly groaned when he moved his leg. He limped over to a table with his drink. He pulled off his bandage, then poured part of his drink on the rag before he tied it back on his leg. The big man grimaced in pain from the alcohol on his wound.

Mekan stepped next to Urith as he paid the owner for his drink and room.

"Do you always fight when you enter a tavern?"

Urith looked at her. The woman's expression betrayed an interest and wariness at the same time.

"Warriors live by a code and I don't back down from a fight," he tied to his money bag to his belt. After several attempts, he just shoved the draw strings into his waist belt.

"Why did you come back so soon?" He asked as he picked up his drink.

"I came out of the temple when Jarra, the tavern owner, ran by me. I figured you were involved when he said there was a fight." Mekan shrugged. "I guess I got curious about what might happen."

"Well, thank you for joining in. We're even now, but Hera won't like you hanging around with me. I believe he has ideas about you." He downed his heathmead.

"That's not your concern," she huffed. Mekan noticed Urith's grimace when he went to retrieve his bags and blanket from the counter. Impatiently, she intervened.

"Come on, I'll help you carry these."

The Esterblud nodded his thanks, then he took his helmet. After attaching it to his belt, he went over to the table where Yartha sat. He gingerly pulled out his spear from the floor. He glanced at the tip.

"Mekan didn't jab my spear tip too deep into your leg. But make sure you clean that wound. We don't need a one-legged fighter when we take on the Borrs."

Yartha leaned back against the table as he studied Urith. The man's calculating thoughts were obvious on his broad face. He grinned with an infectious smile.

"You're an interesting warrior, but don't worry about me, Esterblud. I can keep up with any man that you can find. My wound will heal better than that scar you carry." He laughed at his own joke.

Urith turned away. "I hope that your fighting skills are better than your jokes. By the way, I've heard others remark about my face." He stopped and glared back at Yartha.

"They're dead!"

Yartha's expression remained smug, but he said nothing. Mekan joined the warrior as he took a clay lamp hanging by the stairs.

"I suppose you're friends with the man now, even though he just tried to kill you."

Urith looked back at Yartha who remained focused on his leg wound.

"Like you mentioned earlier, I'm a strange one."

~~~

In a small room above the tavern's first floor, Urith sat at a bench by the entrance. A tattered brown cloth curtain acted as the door while a single window, partially covered with a leather parchment, let in an evening breeze. The warrior pointed to the uncomfortable bed next to him, where Mekan placed his rolled-up blanket and bag. After sitting the oil lamp next to him, Urith unhooked his belts. Gingerly pulled off his tunic. Then, he did the same with his chain mail and padded undershirt. Mekan stood by the bed, undecided whether to leave or stay. What she saw bothered her. Even though Urith appeared close to her age, he carried many scars on his broad chest and arms. The woman heard tales of the Esterbluds passion for violence and the warrior confirmed it. When she thought about his earlier actions, Mekan concluded Urith carried a death wish. Still, the woman saw something in his eyes that she recognized. Agonizing memories brought about by the death of someone close to him. While she'd only
~~~

known Urith for part of the day, the hints in their conversation told her that the man understood her suffering.

As he probed his injured arm, Urith grunted. Mekan came closer and saw an impressive dark blue splotch on his arm where the mace struck.

"Is it broken?"

"I don't think so, but it hurts like *Phlege* fire," he replied while carefully opening and closing his hand. "A night of rest should heal me enough."

Mekan gave him a dubious look but said nothing. Almost on cue, they heard a heavy snoring coming from somewhere down the narrow hallway. She removed his leather bag and unrolled the blanket on the bed. Two spears and the captured weapons from the Borrs were inside.

"Do you warriors always carry so many arms?" Mekan joked as she put them on the bench beside the warrior.

Urith leaned back against the wall.

"They're tools of trade and status. It's the same as farmers who have the best bred ossane or when they build a wooden plow for their field." He remained serious as he watched her.

"There's only one bed."

She ignored him. "Now lay down here."

Urith let out a breath and went to the bed. The hard leather straps that supported his blanket felt like wood as he laid back. He saw her close the curtain.

"It's cheaper for me to stay with you." Mekan unhooked her belt and quickly disrobed. Her shivering, naked body absorbed his thoughts.

Neither of them heard the soft plodding of footsteps came down the hallway. Suddenly, Dutra let himself into the room. He smiled at the woman, who automatically grabbed her clothes. Her face turned red with embarrassment.

"I'm finished. Jarra said you were up here. You owe me a koinon?"

Urith scowled at the intruder, then fumbled for his moneybag on the bench. He tossed the gold coin to him.

"Get out!"

While looking over Mekan with a mischievous grin, the young man looked over the coin. He whistled as he went away.

Urith looked back at Mekan. After a moment, she grinned, and he laughed. The woman dropped her clothes on the floor, then leaned over Urith.

"I don't want to think tonight. I need to forget," Mekan explained as she helped him pull off his leather breeches.

~~~

Urith woke to the early morning light as dawn approached. The warrior felt Mekan tightly snuggled on one side of him. Her peaceful breathing comforted him. However, the sound of someone else sleeping came from the bench near his head. He looked over and saw a curled-up Dutra lying on his side. The extinguished oil lamp rested near the boy's head at the end of the bench. Urith's weapons and clothes were on the floor.

He's like a litta! Urith decided.

The boy reminded him of a worm that attached to a body to suck blood. With a scowl, the warrior woke Mekan. Her initial smile faded when she saw his dark expression. She looked over to where Urith pointed.

"I should have let him starve," he whispered with a sneer.

~~~

Urith and Dutra followed Mekan to the blacksmith's hut after they dressed. The warrior forced the youth to carry his bag and the bandit's weapons. While the young man complained at first, Urith reminded him that food came with work.

"You're the one who asked to become a servant to me," the warrior glared. "I'll show you how to become a warrior, but you must learn to work first." He shifted the weight of the weapons for the boy. Dutra's grumbling stopped, but he wasn't pleased trying to handle the cumbersome load.

For his part, the Esterblud was happy not to carry the extra load. Pain remained with his injured arm, although it lessened after a couple of heathmeads on an empty stomach.

After they reached the blacksmith agreed to purchase the weapons after hard negotiation. Urith took the money, which he split with Mekan.

"I'll have to ride with you to make my koinons," she joked, as they left for the execution.

As the trio stepped into the road, a line of Rarfell guards passed by on their lightly armored ossanes. They went through the main gates in a hurry, which surprised Urith. He guessed they might have heard that the Borrs were somewhere close by. The warrior hoped that

The home of the King Renni wasn't what Urith expected. No grand staircase or marble columns. Instead, a modest two-story wooden building faced them. White paint stood in the place of a stone façade, and the only luxury appeared to be the small windows of colored glass. As the group went through an open area between the barracks and building to find the parade grounds that extended to the walls of the town. A balcony on the side of the modest palace overlooked the grounds where an early crowd gathered. Mekan headed directly to Hera.

Urith remained in the background. The woman needed to know her father's killer had died for his crimes. As he led

Dutra to a place to watch the executions, he heard a familiar voice behind him.

"You Esterbluds recruit your men young and starving."

Yartha limped next to the warrior. His pockmarked face remained stoic, but the man's green eyes twinkled.

"At least you will not hang with those Borrs this morning. I see you joined your kingdom's cause." Urith glanced over. Their contest the night before left him with a favorable impression of the man's natural fighting skills. Still, he wondered about the man's background.

Urith's attention turned to the sound of the three prisoners in chains coming from out of their underground cells near the barracks. With iron bracelets attached to chains that barely reached their leg irons, the three tattooed men shuffled to the gallows while hunched over from their bound hands tied to their knees. When they reached the wood platform, the guards put a noose around the condemned men's necks and hoisted individually on top of an empty heathmead barrel.

Urith noticed Hera escorted Mekan close to the bandit involved in her father's death. Then Hera ordered the guards to tighten the ropes around the condemned prisoners. Mekan suddenly cursed the thug, who no longer carried his smirk. The prisoner finally understood death awaited him. A few within the crowd joined the woman as they heckled the condemned as well. The Esterblud recognized the swaying and overly loud laughs of many drunken men and women who made up the bulk of the crowd closest to the hanging platform.

Then an attendant bellowed from the nearby balcony.

"Our overlord condemns these bandits to death for their crimes against him and those of Rarfell! Let this serve as a warning to others who cross the King."

Urith looked up to see the Rarfell king sitting in an unadorned chair next to his attendant. The man's thin, pale face showed no little emotion at the scene below. Covered in a purple blanket, the king nodded to the guards.

One by one, the guards kicked the barrels from under the feet of the condemned. Each man dropped a bit, then immediately kicked and jerked frantically. Eyes bulging and mouths open, the prisoner's faces contorted into unending expressions of fear, disbelief, and hopelessness. Their chains clinked and rattled with each spasm and movement that only slowly dissipated. Some in the hushed crowd whispered as the first prisoner quite moving. The second one to die was the man Urith captured. A small cheer erupted from Mekan, followed by those people standing close to her. The last man to die caused the rest of the crowd to cheer. Even Dutra joined in the celebration. The boy noticed only Urith stood still as he stared at the swaying dead men.

"Didn't they deserve it?" Dutra asked.

"Of course they did. But there's no glory in dying like a worm on a hook."

"Is there a good way to die?" Yartha interjected. Urith glanced over, expecting the man was joking. He was wrong.

"Yes, dying in battle, for one. I would raise a glass of heathmead with my father in Haligulf."

Yartha smirked at the idea. "Maybe, but I'm only interested if there are plenty of fair maidens who serve me in Haligulf. Someone like this fine one who has eyes for me."

Mekan overheard the remark, and she gave the big man a withering stare.

"Don't flatter yourself!" She turned to Urith. "I'm going to the temple. Maybe this time I can make my offerings for my father without you interrupting me."

She watched Dutra hurry away to watch the guards as they pulled down the bandit's bodies.

Most of the crowd remained, but their attention focused on two men wearing dark robes. The men carried out a wooden slab which looked like a door.

"It appears the entertainment will soon start," Mekan told Urith. "They're putting out the targets for the archery and knife throwing competition."

More attendants and guards soon joined the first two men, adding more targets and stepping off the distances. The entire process appeared well composed. Urith commented on the procession. Yartha grunted.

"Wait until you see the opening."

Mekan smiled and told Urith she was leaving for the temple.

"Stay out of fights," she warned.

"I give no promises," Urith grinned.

Chapter 2: The Killing of a King

While Urith and Yartha watched the activities, they didn't see Rech approaching. The mear called over Hera who hurried over. The two men called out for the fighters of the new company to join them. Slowly, nine men gathered around. What Urith saw in the men was not encouraging. Dressed in the robes and tunics of various clans outside of Rarfell, the mercenaries were a motley crew. The leather breast plates on many of the men wore were their only piece of armor. A few short swords provided the weapons for some, while most carried a single spear along with a bow. Several of the fighters held clay mugs filled with barkmead and swayed while standing around. Urith believed they seldom left the confines of the local drinking establishment.

"I've seen this type of men before," he growled under his breath to Yartha. "They're brawlers among themselves, only here to drink and take loot from the villagers. We'll be lucky that they don't run away at the first sign of fighting."

"Did you expect anything different? People are driven by greed or lust."

Urith looked over.

"Don't forget honor," he said.

"I disagree. You lust to die. You said so last night. There's a difference. Honor is something you tell yourself." Yartha glanced over at the tall woman in the golden dress who came their way. Her alabaster complexion and russet red hair stood out among the many dark-haired people in the crowd. The two guards with her tried to keep up with the woman's long strides.

"You know nothing of my motives. I would ask, why are you here? I don't think you're afraid of Heka's threats." Urith followed his stare. The woman lifted her dress while she avoided a stagnate puddle of mud and water. Her uncovered legs caught the attention of the rest of the men.

"Maybe I'm here because I'm bored with starting fights in the taverns," Yartha grinned. "However, things are looking up now that I've joined this company."

"Everyone in a line," Hera ordered. "Queen Darrca wishes to talk to our volunteers."

Grudgingly, the men formed a haphazard line while talking and laughing. Queen Darrca looked over at each man as she passed by. Urith caught a hint of doubt in the woman's expression. He gave a sly grin that her perception matched his own about some mercenaries. Rech and Hera joined her, and she nodded to them.

"I see you have men to help with your duties. I trust they can remove the Borrs." Her tone matched the suspicion in her eyes.

"Yes, they will provide reinforcements for our guard," Rech quickly explained. The man glanced over at Urith and he pointed at the Esterblud.

"In fact, one of these men already captured a bandit who we executed this morning. He's the one I told the king about."

The queen looked over at the big Esterblud, then came toward the warrior. Rech introduced Urith, who bowed slightly. Her piercing, light blue eyes lit up as she looked over his scar, which surprised him. Usually, the person avoided looking at his face.

"Scarred warrior, I've heard of you. Although, I'm surprised that you brought a prisoner with you. From the tales, I expected you to be double your size with a massive sword in each hand." She stepped back and looked him over. "By the way the skalds spoke about your deeds, I expected you carried the heads of your enemies dangling from to your belt.”

Laughter broke out at the queen's jest. Urith grinned.

“Yes, someone pays them well to give such boasts about me. However, the skalds forget to tell you I eat my enemy's flesh as well.” He heaved a dramatic sigh. “You can't rely on them sometimes.”

Darrca laughed, her smile dazzling the warrior.

“Well, bring more of our enemies to the scaffold, and you'll find my people are quite generous.” She glanced back at the attendants standing by the nearby table.

“Urith, are you taking part in our tournament?”

The warrior shook his head.

“That's too bad.” She frowned and turned away.

His eyes followed her. The queen went to the table which had throwing knives laid out. She picked up three knives and, in quick succession, Darrca sent the knives into the target set several paces away. All three embedded into the middle of the target.

The guards and the men of the new Cymeer Company gave a rousing cheer at the display. As the queen walked away, she confidently nodded, briefly basking in their approval. All eyes followed the woman as she went to the platform where her husband watched.

“She can throw a knife better than any man in her kingdom. She's won the tournaments before,” Rech told Urith when he saw the Esterblud watching the queen.

“Now, there's a woman,” Yartha whistled while he glanced at the king. “With her sickly husband, I'll bet that she needs a guy to keep her happy at night. I wonder which of the guards gets that job.” The man grinned at Rech's obvious disapproval of his thoughts.

"She's not a usual noble," Urith nodded with obvious admiration.

Rech clapped his hands to get the line of men's attention.

"For those who wish to battle, you will soon have your chance. You are the first fighters in our new Cymeer Company. Tomorrow morning, the company will leave for Eleb where Rarfell guards will train and guide you as you clear our lands of the enemy. Enjoy the festivities."

The mear scowled at Yartha as he left the area.

"I'll be leading you men to Eleb," Hera spoke. "We leave when the sun rises in the west. Make sure your weapons are sharp and their ossanes are ready." He looked over at Yartha. "Make sure you can ride. I've seen your limp. We don't need you slowing us down."

The tavern thug grinned at Hera. "I'll keep up with you any day. Just give me an ossane."

As the new company of fighters broke up, Urith paid little attention. He kept watching Darrca. When she took a seat next to her husband, the queen watched the group of men now called the Cymeer Company. It appeared they were discussion her thoughts about the mercenaries. He wondered if Darrca agreed with the king's strategy.

"Lerah left with the guards going to Eleb this morning," Yartha's voice seemed to respond to Urith's thoughts. "Rumor says that Lerah has a hunger for the throne and his sister tried to make him regent for the sick king. Renni made him head of the guard instead. I can't say that was a smart move."

Urith glanced over, suddenly wondering more about his new comrade. As a tavern thug, Yartha carried an unusual interest in knowing the rumors and happening of royal intrigues. The two men watched with interest as the king suddenly broke out into a coughing fit. After a while, Renni retreated from the platform with the help of his aides. The queen and her brother took over as the competition on the field below started.

Urith noticed a wagon pull into the field, close to the gallows. As a crowd gathered around, a portly man jumped down. Urith overheard the man apologized for his tardiness.

"Cursed guards went through my cart like I'm a thief," he complained. "Gather around for the best heathmead in Rarfell."

With the help of several thirsty men who hauled the casks to the gallows' platform, the trader soon opened the small barrels of drink.

"Well, my throat is dry," Urith said with a grin. Yartha blurted out a laugh and limped with him to the wagon.

Before long, the two men sat on the back of the wagon with clay mugs in their hands. The men made a deal with the trader to watch over his goods in return for a place to sit and watch the events in the field. After several rounds of drink, Urith focused on the men involved in the archery competition. Their skills with a bow reminded him of stories about the dreaded *fealharn*. A skald once told him he saw one of the renowned assassins place an arrow through a man's eye at one hundred paces. While Urith had his doubts at the claim, the man in the archery competition was deadly accurate at fifty paces. The lean man with a long beard wearing a brown robe of a trader appeared out of place among the other competitors. He mentioned his observation to Yartha.

"We should take some of those men with us," the Esterblud wiped the heathmead suds from his lips with his sleeve. "The rain of arrows on a battlefield can turn the tide in our favor."

Yartha farted with a smile, then shook his head lazily.

"You act like there are techniques to battles and fighting. It's just a massive brawl. I like brawls."

"You won't think that when a line of armored ossanes comes at you with a wall of spears." Urith replied, then finished his drink. Like Yartha, he felt the effects of the drink.

"We need to find food or this heathmead will send us to the ground," he said.

Yartha laughed.

"Then we go to the tavern of the Rarfell guards. I want to see them throw out a member of the Cymeer Company." He slid off the wagon and held himself steady by holding on to the side of the cart.

With a sodden grin, Urith joined him. He looked over as the crowd of spectators let out a roar when the bearded archer won the competition. The Esterblud notice a blue tattoo under the man's sleeve.

"He must come from a mountain tribe. I'd like to see his tattoo." Urith pointed to the man.

"Why? Do you need one for yourself? Come on, it's time for food," Yartha belched. Urith grinned and the two men staggered across the field in the general direction of the road.

"You're not of this kingdom. What brings you here?" Urith asked.

Yartha's eyes narrowed, and he looked over at the warrior.

"What makes you think I'm not from Cymeer?"

"You have a dagger with the marking of a Gallaeci tribe. I've seen them before."

"I could have taken it from a dead man."

"Perhaps, but I hear a hint of dialect in your words as well. I've traded with Gallaeci many times and I notice the weapons that people carry."

"I'll remember that," Yartha grumbled. "Yes, I'm from Ynyover. Came from a small village on the other side of the highlands. I arrived here during the last festivals and stayed. I've left for koinons a few times, but I always come back here."

When the two men entered the tavern across from the barracks, the owner gave Yartha a withering glare. Urith grunted at his new friend's reputation. In Esterblud, thugs seldom hung around places where warriors gathered. It wasn't healthy for them to start fights with well-armed men. Urith placed a couple of coins on the wood counter and the tavern owner's sour expression transformed into a smile.

"We need erba meat and lots of it," the Esterblud said too loudly for the empty room.

~~~

The Kamin sun reached its zenith when Dutra found the two men. They were relaxing on the front steps of the tavern after a heavy meal and more drinks. The buzz of alcohol still wafted through Urith's mind, but he was no longer staggering. The boy insisted Urith join him, so he finally followed Dutra to a building where Mekan waited.

"I wanted to talk with you before you leave," she explained. The woman dismissed the youth with a glance, and she led the warrior around the side of the structure.

"I'm trying to determine my next steps. I don't want to return to the farm. There are too many memories there."

Urith nodded as they walked through the knee-high bluish *ikal* grass. He guessed that, without a family, Mekan sought advice from someone she trusted.

"I don't know what I'll do. If I return, my uncle will wish to marry me and take over the land."

She paused.
~~~

"I spoke with Rech. He advised me to marry my uncle. He explained how such an arrangement fixes all my problems, a stable life as a farm wife." Mekan looked over at Urith. "It's nothing I wish to do. I have other plans."

"A pretty girl like you must have admirers. What about Hera?"

She blushed and nodded.

"I thought about him. Even though he knows I stayed with you, he would take me. But I seek someone who looks for adventure and travel." She stopped when they came to a slow-moving creek. Her hand took his.

"You find me attractive. Even with the wound on your face, you carry a confidence I find appealing. Rech states you are a natural leader for the Cymeer Company they plan to build. You need someone."

Urith turned the woman to face him.

"You're a fine woman with the smarts and looks to make any man proud. Such an arrangement might work for a while, but I'm not the one you need. Eventually, I will return to Esterblud. From there, who knows where I will travel? It is not good for you."

"That's not the only reason." Mekan frowned.

The Esterblud nodded.

"No, I've had another woman who thought like you. However, the scar I carry remains inside. It is deep and the visions at night still hurt me."

The woman stared into his eyes.

"I thought so. Her name came out as you slept. Can you get over her?"

"Sell the land, take your bag of koinons and run away," Urith suggested, evading her question. "My guess is that Hera would probably follow along."

She gave a half-smile at the thought. "You don't know him. Rarfell carries a loyalty to the land and the family. Things aren't done like that. Besides, where would I go and what would I do?"

"That's up to you, isn't it?"

Mekan frowned.

"An unarmed woman traveling our lands is a death wish. Perhaps you can take me when you leave?"

"Are you that unhappy in Rarfell? Or is this something else? In the short time I've known you, you've spoken of no dreams." Urith kneeled by the water's edge. He broke a stick from the limb of dead bush next to him and threw it in the water. After a moment, Mekan joined him.

"I'm afraid. I've never been on my own. I'm grasping for something." She broke a piece of the limb, then poked it into the mud by her feet. "You know, a caravan of Gallaeci came by our farm when I was younger. Of course, my father told me about the Gallaeci's terrible ways. However, I couldn't keep the image of wandering the lands like a Gallaeci do out of my mind." Mekan looked over at Urith.

"Why should men decide my life? Am I to grow old seeing nothing beyond the borders of this land?" She threw her stick into the water.

Urith thought about Yartha's admission, and he couldn't help but grin at the irony.

"Why do you smile?"

The warrior took a deep breath.

"Because I sometimes make rotten decisions." He glanced over. "When I'm through with my time here, I can take you to Eran. It's the gateway to all the kingdoms."

Mekan momentarily smiled at the thought.

"Is a warrior always sympathetic to the worries of a simple farm girl?"

Urith rose and reached out with his hand. He grimaced when he helped her back up. He flexed the complaining muscles of his injured arm.

"No, but I'm selfish enough to enjoy a warm body next to me at night. It helps me sleep." Urith spanked her lightly on the rear as they walked back to the village.

~~~

Late in the evening, two naked lovers dozed in the cramped bed. Both heard a man yell a warning in the darkness. The sound of his frantic voice suddenly cutoff. Instantly, Urith got out of bed. The tense feeling in the air had him scrambling to get on his clothes. His movements woke Mekan.

"Look out the window," he ordered the woman. "See what's happening."

"Get off my chain mail," Urith ordered Dutra, who charged out of the small room.

"I can't see anything outside. There are hardly any lamps burning." The woman stretched her head through the window.

"Never mind, just get your clothes on. Something is going on and I don't like it."

A moment later, a terrified scream confirmed Urith's concerns. A dull, red glowing light came through the window. Half dressed, Mekan looked out to see a building on fire toward the screams. She saw a couple escaping from the building. But they ran into men who killed them instantly. Mekan hurried to the door.

"We have to escape. I've seen men with weapons coming this way."

Urith slid on his baudrik belt, then his helmet. He left his boots but grabbed his circular shield.
~~~

"They better enjoy my blade," he growled as he pulled his Clovel sword.

They reached the bottom of the stairs, where Dutra rushed up.

"Men overwhelmed the guards at the gate. They have tattoos like those men the king hung," he panted out. The boy looked over as Yartha came into the building. He held a flask in his hand, appearing unperturbed by the growing chaos outside.

"You might want to join us," Urith told him before he turned back to Dutra.

"You and Mekan find a place to hide by the stables. I'll come for you if we have to leave in a hurry."

"What are you planning?" Yartha's eyes gleamed as he sat his flask on top of the bar. He slid his heavy mallet from his belt.

"We head to the overlord's house and the barracks. The invaders will head there." The Esterblud headed to the door.

"What if someone already overran the guards?" Yartha asked when they reached the street.

Urith didn't bother to answer as he hurried in bare feet toward a small group of men waiting at the entrance of a building. Even in the dull light, the warrior recognized the tattooed faces. Urith struck down the Borr who turned toward him. He recovered in time to deflect the spear thrust at him with his shield. The Clovel sword cut through the enemy's leather helmet, sending the dying Borr to the ground. Yartha joined the battle with a vicious swing of his mallet into the shield of another Borr who backed away. Yartha followed him into the shadows. Urith glanced over to see the last bandit run off into the shadows.

"Come on," he huffed to Yartha as the man came back into view. "To the barracks."

The two men hurried down the dark street, pausing at the edge of each building. Occasionally, they came upon bodies of butchered townspeople. As the men drew closer, the fire from the barracks was already covering the thatched roof.

"Rarfell is falling," Yartha yelled out. "I see men over by the king's quarters."

Urith immediately changed direction. When he reached the entrance to the front, the Esterblud slammed his shield into the back of a Borr bandit standing in his way. The man fell to the floor and Urith thrust his sword blade into the prostrate enemy as he passed. Urith heard a melee coming from the second floor. He hurried up the stairs to find a massive man in heavy armor, along with several more men at the end of the hall. They were attacking two Rarfell guards standing in front of a door.

The leader swung his mallet and one of the defending guard's shield shattered from the impact. The guard yelled out in pain while his companion went down from two thrusting spears impaling his middle.

"Phillo demands the king fight him," the leader of the bandits yelled as he swung his mallet. The heavy iron slammed into the silver helmet of the injured guard. Blood and brain splattered as the Regia guard's head collapsed like rotten fruit.

As Urith started forward, a hand grabbed Urith's shoulder.

"Come with me!" Hera dragged the Esterblud through a curtain as the Borrs pressed their attack.

Urith followed him along with Yartha, who saw Hera pull the Esterblud into the back stairway. Urith noticed the blood on Hera's helmet and ripped clothes. The Rarfell Guard carried a short sword and his shield. He quickly led the men down the wooden stairs to a back room on the main floor. They entered the large kitchen area where the king and queen stood with several of their unarmed retainers.

"We're going across the courtyard. I need both of you to draw these bandits away from the king and queen." Hera hurriedly told them.

A death cry came down the passageway from above. The crash of a door followed.

"Get those cursed retainers armed and go," Urith growled as he crossed the room. He slid several large knives across a table to the men in colorful robes. Urith was already at the back door when the queen took a knife from her aide. At the door, the warrior glanced over at the sickly king, who held a short sword with a dazed expression.

Hera pushed Yartha to the back door as they joined the Esterblud.

"Renni, follow us, and we'll get you to the safety of the stables. Urith, you bring up the rear."

The small group hurried out of the door. A pale-yellow light from the burning barracks made it easy for them to see where they were going. It also allowed the Borrs to spot them. Cries and yells filled the air behind them as the king's entourage reached the mear's home. They quickly entered the house.

On the stairs lay a blood covered woman, still in her linen underclothes and clutching her belly. The king began coughing as he passed by. His wife covered her mouth, then she stopped to reach down and help.

"She's dead, keep moving," Urith gruff voice caught her attention. Then he called out.

"Hera, you find a way out back."

The Esterblud looked back into the street where armed men hurried toward their location. Darrca tried to look past him.

"Get to the back and follow Hera," Urith ordered the queen quietly. Darrca glared at him.

"What are doing?"

"I'll keep your enemies busy!" He gave her his sneer grin.

The queen left him as the Esterblud quietly chanted an homage to the *Estercetus*, a sea serpent creature who helped protect his tribe. He backed away from the door, waiting for the first bandit to enter. The warrior heard his comrades quietly leaving the house.

Outside, the sound of footsteps slowed as men got to the front of the building. Urith overheard a rough sounding voice ordering some men to go around to the back. The Esterblud suddenly dragged his sword across the floor. The noise sent bandits rushing through the front door.

Urith made the first man pay for his mistake with a wide sweep of his sword. The Borr's head flipped away and rolled across the floor. The bandit following him tripped over the body. As Urith thrust his heavy sword into the man, a mallet flew through the door. The weapon struck Urith in his shoulder before striking his helmet. The force of the blow sent the warrior out of the entrance. Almost immediately, the hulking leader of the Borrs entered the room.

"Find the king and kill this Esterblud," Phillo bellowed out.

Shaking his head from the stunning blow, Urith backed away as more bandits pushed into the room. One of the Borrs thrust a spear at Urith, who barely avoided the tip.

Just keep them interested in me!

"Is that the best you calwards can do?" Urith growled as he spun into the next room. The Borrs loudly cursed as they came after him. Urith scrambled through the backdoor, hoping more of the enemy weren't waiting for him. Once outside, the warrior could see nothing in the shadows of the building. However, he heard the noise of men coming around the corner from one side and Urith went in the opposite direction. He heard the shouts of the bandits as they continued to follow.

Urith turned a corner and waited for a moment as the sound of heavy boots and clanging weapons moved in another direction. After catching his breath, the warrior started working his way through the shadows. He was heading in the direction of the ossane stables.

I hope Hera got the king and queen out of Cymeer!

It took a while before Urith got close to the stables. When he rounded the corner, he saw a bloody fight occurring under the light of lamps. Two of the Rarfell Guards stood with Hera to protect King Renni. Urith witnessed a retainer standing by the king fall with an arrow to the neck. Bandits attacked Hera and his guards with swords. Nearby, Yartha held off a Borr who attacked the queen.

Running across the open ground, Urith slammed his shield into the back of the first bandit in his way. His attack distracted the Borrs from fighting the king. Hera took down one with a strike on his enemy's leg. However, their partial success was short-lived. More bandits arrived, led by Phillo.

"Get to the ossanes," Hera cried to his king.

Urith got close to Yartha, who had trouble in his fight with one of the enemy fighters. Urith ran behind the Borr fighting Yartha and impaled the man in the back. Then, the Esterblud called out for Dutra and Mekan. However, they didn't respond.

Urith saw Darrca stab her knife into an enemy warrior who grabbed her. The Esterblud rushed over and swung his Clovel sword into the back of the queen's attacker. After the man fell, he grabbed Darrca and manhandled her to the fence that held the ossanes. Yartha scrambled over the rails as Urith nearly threw the woman into the pen. Nervous ossanes pranced and snorted behind the fence.

"Get her on one mount," Urith ordered Yartha before he turned back to help Hera and the king.

In the dim light, Phillo's size and helmet stood out among the rushing onslaught of fighters. The leader of the Borrs wore a bone-colored helmet that looked like a human skull coming down over his eyes. His metal armor extended across his broad shoulders and attached to a breastplate with the symbol of the Gallaeci. When he reached Hera, Phillo swung his mallet into the man's shield, sending the guard backward. The action left King Renni exposed, and several men drew back their bows. The flight of arrows slammed into the man's body just as Urith arrived. The Esterblud swung at Phillo, who felt the Clovel Sword cut into his gauntlet. The Borr leader backed away, pulling his broad sword into his other hand.

As Hera tried to drag his overlord away, a thrown spear pierced the dying king. He grunted before blood poured out of his mouth. With more of the bandits came out of the darkness at them, Hera released his grip on the king. He and Urith backed away, trying to avoid the thrown spears. One struck Urith's shield, partially embedding into the wood.

"Let's get the queen out of here!" Hera gasped out. The winded warriors hurried to the ossane pen while the Borrs descended around the body of King Renni.

Urith slammed into a bandit who arrived out of the darkness. His shield left the stunned man on the ground. Hera grabbed a lit oil lamp from a post and unhooked the entrance gate to the pen.

Arrows and spears fell around the men as Urith pushed by the Rarfell guard. Hera swung his lamp into the Borrs who followed. The clay body struck the ground and flames covered the area. Oily flames climbed on a man who screamed as he tried to beat out the fire.

Urith reached Yartha and Darrca who were already on ossanes. He jumped behind the queen as Hera opened the gate. Without hesitation, Yartha spurred his mount and took off. Darrca followed him.

As the riders came out of the corral, they witnessed Phillo remove the head of Renni with a swing of his sword. Several of the Borrs attempted to intercept the escaping riders. Yartha swung at the first bandit, missing him, but he forced the man out of their way by using his mount as a battering ram. His action allowed the queen's ossane to pass. Arrows peppered the area as they hurried toward the front gate.

When they reached the entrance to the fortress town, only a few of the bandits stood in their way. Unprepared for the escaping ossanes, the Borrs scrambled to stop them. Urith sliced through the upper body of the man in their way. With a groan, the man swung around in a strange pirouette before falling dead. An instant later, the two ossanes galloped into the night.

~~~

It was nearly morning when the three escapees from Cymeer finally came to a stop. They found an abandoned hut close to the main road. The shack still had most of the
~~~

thatched roof left and a few bits of mostly broken furniture. Grass grew on the dirt floor.

As Yartha built a fire in the fireplace, Urith led the ossanes to a nearby creek for water. He left the animals tied to a tree.

"We can only rest for a short time. Those bandits will follow us in their search for the queen." Urith told them as he returned.

Darrca sat on a wooden stool that Yartha found.

"We'll need to find food and water," Urith continued as he crouched by the fire. He looked down at his bare feet, which hurt. "Boots for me as well. Curse, I wish I had more time to bring Dutra and Mekan along."

"We could use saddles and another ossane as well," Yartha stated. "Where are we going to find these things?"

"This road leads to Cahmais. I say we take the next road to Esterblud. Safety for the Darrca lays in Jarma. It's a small village just across the border. I don't think the Borrs want to risk King Penhda's involvement." Urith looked over at the queen, who appeared lost in her own thoughts.

"Gallaeci controls the village. Are you just avoiding Cahmais because they are the mortal enemy of Esterbluds? After all, they might decide to hang you if you go into their kingdom." Yartha pulled out his mallet and slid the face across the ground as if to clean it. Urith didn't see any blood on it. Then he slid the weapon back into his belt. Yartha noticed Urith's expression.

"I listen to the skalds when they come through Cymeer," he shrugged.

"Cahmais has good relations with the king of Rarfell," Darrca interjected. She pushed her long hair out of her face as she considered her options. "I've heard that Asgurd enjoys a solid relationship with the Sacred Overlord as well. Satres and Asgurd supporting my claim is useful."

"I recommend that you don't do that. You are allowing the Aberffraw warriors into your land. King Penhda will not take such actions lightly," the Esterblud warned her.

"I like parts of your plan, Urith. To rebuild an army to retake the kingdom makes sense." Her eyes were bright with hatred. "But I'm hesitant about going into another kingdom. It sounds like I'm running away."

"Once I get to Esterblud, I will go to King Pendha. He will offer help, I'm sure." Urith assured her. "Phillo's head will rest on a spike in front of the gatehouse door."

"I want him and the Borrs to suffer far more than a quick death." The woman lashed out.

There was an awkward silence.

"It's a shame that Hera didn't try to escape with us," the queen finally said.

"He made the right decision," Urith grunted. "Without his help, you'd probably be the captive of the Borrs. I understand your regret for I left two people in Cymeer. I need to go back to help them."

"Hera is a brave man. He's from the tribe of Cyer, ancient warriors who ruled the valley. He's a distant relation of my family. My husband put him into the role on the advice of Rech." She paused, remembering the death of Renni. "I must rule wisely, like the king."

"After the fight that King Renni put up, he now stands among the heroes within Haligulf," Urith assured her.

"I'm sure," she replied diplomatically, then paused.

"My husband was a smart man, but not an influential leader. The arranged marriage between king and queen kept our two tribes strong enough to avoid such invasions in the past. But our clans grew weak when the Gallaeci first came to our land. Their people act as traders, then seek to overwhelm our villages with rabble."

She didn't see Yartha's frown at the comment.

"I must contend with the Borrs who come on our land from various paths, including areas of your kingdom. Rech insisted we attack them while the king's health made such ideas impractical. The queen's brother, Lerah, worked with the king and Rech to bring about the Cymeer Company into place. I hoped Renni would name Lerah as regent, but the king remained stubbornly against the idea." She sighed. "I don't enjoy the politics and tribal alliances necessary to rule a kingdom. Maybe I deferred that too much to Lerah and Rech."

The queen stared into the flames of the fire.

"Now, the mountains bleed the blood of our people. I've heard stories about the Borrs as they continued to sweep in, then leave. My husband believed they were scavengers who will run back across the mountains once Rarfell men fought them. If I only had a spot inside the kingdom to gather those who remain loyal. I guess I have no option."

The woman straightened when she realized Urith carefully watched her while remaining silent.

"Urith, I realize how much I owe you and your friend." She smiled, then looked at Yartha. "I should have asked before. What is your name?"

The man scowled momentarily, then he introduced himself to her. When he mentioned he was from the Gallaeci tribe, both men noticed the queen's expression darkened slightly at the news. Darrca glanced away momentarily.

"When we reach Esterblud, I'd consider it an honor for both of you joined my cause," Darrca regained her composure.

"Too bad we don't have heathmead to toast the idea," Yartha smiled broadly. "My queen, I had a thought about something you said earlier. Rech told us that the Rarfell Guard went to Eleb. It is close to this road we take. We should go there first."

He looked over at Urith.

"The Rarfell warriors might be strong enough to help us," Yartha insisted. "Plus, it allows us to get you back to Cymeer sooner."

Urith scowled.

"It's just a small band of guards. They can't stand against the Borrs who gather to come after us."

"Still, they are loyal and trained to fight. What Yartha says makes sense," Darrca conceded. She leaned back against the wall of the hut. The queen looked between the men as she considered the idea.

"It is your decision," Yartha grew excited by his idea. "I'm sure Hera would approve. They are Cyer warriors, after all! They deserve a chance to fight back."

The queen nodded as a pleased expression filled her face.

"Yartha, I'm glad you thought of this. Yes, we must let the Rarfell defenders drive out the enemy. That is my best option. We will go to Eleb!"

"Well, you're the one in charge of these lands." Urith nodded, trying to temper his irritation when the queen overrode his advice.

"We can tell the farmers along the way that you seek all defenders of your kingdom to join you in Eleb." The Esterblud warrior rose. "I'm going to get a drink from the creek and check our ossanes."

Darrca yawned, then nodded. "I think I'll rest before we ride further." The queen crawled over to a relatively soft place on the grass. She lay on her side with her back to the fire.

The twin moons waned in the south when Urith finally came back to the campfire. It took time to move the ossanes to a suitable spot for food and the time allowed him to clear his head. He found Yartha resting against the old chimney. He stared at the sleeping queen while absently drawing figures on the ground with a stick.

"It's too bad I'm not a noble. I'd take her for my wife and become king of this petty little kingdom." Yartha glanced over before returning his eyes to Darrca. His tone and expression revealed the obvious lust for her.

"I don't think she'd have you," Urith joked. "I saw her look change when you told her that you came from the Gallaeci tribe. I don't think her people approve of your people's ways."

"Probably not," Yartha agreed. He leaned over to poke the fire with a stick. "The Gallaeci grow strong knowing everyone treats them as scum."

"Not everyone," the Esterblud leaned back on his saddle. "I've met Gallaeci traders who will give a fair deal on weapons and drink. I hold no grudge against your people."

"Really?" the man looked over skeptically. "You've invited Gallaeci into your village? Drank with them in a tavern?"

Urith gave Yartha his sneer grin.

"Haven't you and I had drinks and fought together?"

"Someday, my clan, along with the others, will rise and destroy our enemies," Yartha stated as he continued to watch the sleeping woman.

~~~

Early the next morning, a cloudy sky threatened rain. Below the king's balcony, the body of King Renni hung by his feet. Stripped of clothes, his emaciated corpse twisted
~~~

slowly in the light morning breeze. Nearby, a captive audience of remaining Cymeer villagers huddled inside a ring of armed Borr men. Phillo stepped out on the platform and looked down upon his new subjects. His heavy armor was gone. He wore a gray broadcloth shirt which hung past his waist. It barely covered his barrel-like chest. He paraded back and forth on the platform with one hand holding a large mug of heathmead. His other hand gripped his mallet.

"My rule over Rarfell starts with sweeping away all rules given by the weak. The world of the Borrs requires absolute obedience to the ways of Facarm."

He stopped and smiled grimly at the quiet crowd watching him. Only the Borrs shouted their approval as Phillo waved his prisoner over. Rech struggled as two Borr thugs pushed the bound man to the edge of the balcony.

"Since your puny overlord died before I could reach him, you will stand in his place." Phillo nodded at the men, who forced Rech to his knees.

The leader of the Borrs took a drink of his heathmead, then raised the mallet above his head. In a quick turn, the heavy iron slammed down on the top of Rech's head. The man's skull collapsed like a shattered egg, splattering blood and tissue across the balcony and into the crowd.

As the Borrs dragged Rech's body away, another bandit pushed Hera to the spot. The Rarfell guard limped from his leg wound, caused by a spear. The bandits overpowered him after the queen escaped, leaving his face and body bruised and battered. Expecting the same treatment as Rech, Hera cursed Phillo.

"The queen will return with an army to mount your head on a pole outside the gates." He growled out before his guard punched the man in the belly.

Phillo laughed at the threat.

"You are a brave one. For your heroic, if futile actions, with the Esterblud last night, I have other plans for you. My *horuks* will soon arrive for my entertainment."

He turned to the crowd.

"You see that my judgment is fair!" the new king of Rarfell yelled out.

"Hang him inside by his thumbs inside my new home until the pen is ready. Bring me the next prisoner for my judgement," Phillo told the captive's guard. As the guard pulled Hera away, the leader of the Borrs looked over his occupied town.

Before long, my new kingdom will know how they submit to Facarm.

Chapter 3: The Road to Eleb

At sunset the next day, the three travelers stopped near the crossroads to Eleb. Moving off the road, they hid their ossanes behind several giant *lellowtere* trees. They carefully walked closer to the tavern where several ossanes stood, tied out front.

"I'll go inside and see who's there. These rural people might notice a queen and a barefoot Esterblud," Yartha joked.

"Alright, you fool, but keep your jokes to yourself. Go back and ride to the building on your ossane. Otherwise, they'll wonder why you're walking," Urith growled at him.

"Yes, father," the Gallaeci replied sarcastically as he hurriedly limped through the brush.

Darrca slid in next to Urith. "I cannot tell whether or not you are friends."

"Neither can I," the Esterblud grunted. "I've only known him for a short time, but it appears we carry similar scars inside."

"Can you trust him? He's a Gallaeci." She paused. "They have a reputation."

"I trust he fought with us and helped you to escape. There's something to be said about that." Urith turned his head to watch Yartha as he passed by on his mount.

"I see you are adept at evading questions. You mentioned two people you left at Cymeer. Were they women you left?"

Urith took a deep breath. "Mekan is the daughter of a farmer killed by the Borrs. I promised to get her to Eran. She wants to see the world. Dutra wanted to be my servant after I caught him trying to steal from me. He's just trying to survive."

The queen tried to read his expression, but the warrior showed her nothing.

"I find it interesting that a warrior cares about two without family. It's…unusual. I've met nobles of Esterblud who traveled to Rarfell. Perhaps I know of your family." Darrca noticed his expression turn dark.

"My father was Uolven. He died during the last Cahmais raids on Esterblud. My older brother, Pehnuwick, is the diplomat in the family."

The queen nodded. "Yes, of course. I met your brother when he came before my husband a few seasons back. King Penhda keeps friendly relations with Rarfell. However, I didn't know of your father's death. You have my sympathy."

Urith glanced at her.

"I appreciate your thoughts. I think that you're an unusual woman."

She smiled. "Why do you say that?"

"Because you are already burdened by your husband's death and now the weight of a kingdom rests on your shoulders." The Esterblud looked away. "Yet, you ask about a stranger's family."

Darrca pursed her lips and turned to look at the tavern. Urith's attention focused on Yartha as he slid off his mount. The oil lamp hanging from the wall showed the man looking over the ossanes tied at the entrance.

"We'll know soon enough if a fight breaks out," he declared as Yartha entered the building.

It wasn't long before the Gallaeci came back out of the tavern with another man who looked familiar to Urith.

"It's my brother!" Darrca rose from their hidden position. She hurried to the tavern.

Urith followed, carefully looking around while he listened to their conversation.

"Lerah, what are you doing here?" The queen asked after her brother bowed to her.

"I was on my way back to Cymeer. Yartha told me of your escape. My dear sister, are you alright?"

Lerah stood tall with a lean body. His oblong face, thin lips and dark eyes were in contrast to his sister's pretty features. He wore a purple robe over his chain mail vest. On top of Lerah's head was a wool bonnet that stretched over his long, blond hair.

"I'm fine," Darrca replied. "It is fortunate you're here. Your guidance is welcome. We must take back the throne."

Lerah took her by the arm. "Come inside. We can discuss the next steps."

When Urith returned with the ossane, they left behind the lellowtere tree, he made a quick inspection of the saddled mounts at the tavern's front porch. He noticed the embedded silver with the symbol of the Rarfell Guards engraved into the metal on one saddle. He tied off his mount and stepped into the quiet building. The low-slung ceiling of the tavern forced Urith to hunch over. He noticed two men sitting in the corner; they paid no attention to the Esterblud coming in the door. Lerah and Darrca sat at a well-used table while Yartha stood at the bar, drinking barkmead. Urith scowled at him, then turned to the fat tavern owner.

"Give me something better than that urine water."

The man grinned and pulled up a large clay container from a back shelf. "It's called *marltal*, nectar of the gods." He placed a wooden cup of the drink in front of Urith.

After a sniff, the Esterblud tasted the sweet-smelling liquid. It reminded him of a heavy Aberffraw wine.

"It'll do!" he grudgingly told the man. He heard his stomach growl.

"How about food as well?"

The warrior looked over at the table, overhearing part of the conversation. He didn't like how loud Lerah spoke.

"Your plan to get Eleb is good. A queen should not abandon her people. You have the guards waiting for your orders." Lerah waved the tavern keeper over. He ordered marltal for the queen.

"I saw you look over the ossanes outside. You must have noticed the Rarfell Guard saddle." Urith looked over at Yartha.

"Yes, then I recognized Lerah." The Gallaeci hesitated. "Of course, he didn't know me."

Urith nodded as he sipped the drink. He kept glancing at the two men sitting in the corner. Dressed in the brown, hooded woolen robes of local herders, the men leaned over their mugs. However, they seldom took drinks from the mugs.

"Something odd about how those men in the corner aren't curious about strangers coming into their tavern." Urith whispered to Yartha.

"I'd be more worried about getting boots and supplies. We won't get to Eleb without food. You need another ossane as well," the Gallaeci tipped back his drink.

Urith nodded as the tavern owner returned. He asked the fat man about supplies.

"We need enough for travel to Eleb."

"Do you have koinons?" There was suspicion in his eyes.

Urith threw pulled two silver pieces from his bag and threw them on the counter.

"We need *erba* meat," the Esterblud said. "Jerky and root tubers for our packs as well."

"I can get those for you. I'll check with my wife about the boots. She trades with customers for food and drink." The tavern owner left through the backdoor. Urith saw him going to a small hut behind the building.

Queen Darrca and her brother approached Urith and Yartha.

"Darrca will travel with me to Eleb in the morning," Lerah told them. "Have the owner bring food to us in my room."

"We have Borrs looking for her. We should continue on to Eleb now." Urith told them.

"I disagree. The queen needs rest. There's no reason to risk her safety by traveling at night." Lerah looked over at his sister. "Besides, no Borr can follow your trail in the dark."

"I agree with my brother." Darrca agreed.

Urith slammed his cup on the counter after finishing the drink. "Then sleep comfortably!" he growled. "I'll have things ready for when we leave." The Esterblud left them and went outside. Darrca stared at the open door.

"Yartha, your friend could learn manners around a queen." Lerah said. "You should mention this to him when he returns." He turned to Darrca.

"Come upstairs, my sister. You need food and rest to keep your strength up for the coming days. Your health is precious to me."

Darrca nodded and went with him to the roughhewn stairs. As they reached the second floor, she looked over at Lerah.

"How do you know Yartha? He's a Gallaeci. You've expressed definite ideas about that tribe."

Lerah's face turned red.

"Well, I've probably spoken too rashly in the past. He mentioned his name when he came to my table. I recognized him since he's a member of the Cymeer Company."

"But you left for Eleb before that happened."

Lerah smiled at her.

"Rech informed me of the people who were coming. You forget I watched you giving your dagger demonstration. Fortunately, the Borrs are nowhere around Eleb."

~~~

Early the next morning, the wind blew cold from the nearby mountains as the Queen and her brother led the riders toward Eleb. Yartha followed the pair closely while Urith brought up the rear, riding an elderly ossane. Yartha appeared interested in the conversations between the royal siblings. For his part, Urith paid little attention. His mind was on keeping his toes warm. On the Esterblud's feet were a well-worn pair of ill-fitting small boots with a large hole cut out in the front of each to accommodate his toes. He was happy that Lerah bought saddles for the ossanes that morning. Riding bareback on the stinking animals caused the leather breeches of a person to carry the same smell wherever they went.

Occasionally, the Esterblud's thoughts came back to something that puzzled him. He was curious about Lerah traveling alone back to Cymeer. It appeared out of character for a person of his status to have no escort with the bandits raiding the countryside. The queen's brother carried only a short sword.

Lerah probably had no choice.

The small kingdom lacked warriors, and they now required mercenaries to help them. The king or his advisors failed to recruit farmer's sons. Many warriors of common stock came from the farms to seek the glory of battle over the drudgery of such hard work.

About mid-day, the riders reached a winding, narrow path that ran along the side of a white chalk cliff face. The road was only wide enough for a single ossane along several
~~~

long stretches of the ride. Along the side of the trail, the blue green *wstinga* brush clung precariously to the torn landscape. Their thorny branches snagging at the legs of the ossanes occasionally.

Several black *vensars* flew overhead, lazily circling while using the air currents. Urith hated the winged scavengers who arrived after battles to feast upon the dead bodies of brave fighters. The steep downward angle on one side of the trail occasionally revealed skeletal remains of erbas and ossanes that slipped off the clay path during rains. Urith assumed some bones mixed with riders who fell with their mounts.

On the other side of the valley, the broken ground showed a recent massive landslide which stretched all the way to the bottom of the ravine. Enormous boulders lay at the bottom, creating a small lake amid the blue green vegetation.

The riders came out of the valley around in the late afternoon, finding a fork in the road. One trail led to Ynyover, while the other went to the last large village in Rarfell. The queen and her brother were a few ossane lengths ahead of Urith and Yartha, who slowed his mount to ride with the Esterblud. As they passed the turn to Ynyover, Urith noticed Yartha glance over.

"Are you still upset the queen decided against your idea?" The Gallaeci shifted in his saddle.

Urith frowned. "No, each idea has merit."

"But she should have deferred to you?" Yartha grinned. "Women should defer to the man."

"Don't put words in my mouth," the Esterblud grunted. "Ideas can come from anyone. At times, my temper gets the best of me."

"So, I see. Still, Eleb holds allies along with food and drink." Yartha remained upbeat. "Besides, we should get the best rooms since we're all that's left of the Cymeer Company. I'm sure the other men in our group fled the capital like we did. Otherwise, they're dead."

Urith wasn't paying attention as he watched many vensars flying over the area where they were heading.

"I just hope we have enough men to go back to Cymeer soon," Yartha continued. "I'm sure you want to see that pretty farmer girl again." He scowled when he realized Urith kept watching the sky ahead of them. The Gallaeci glanced toward the soaring birds.

"I wonder what they see?" Urith commented. Yartha just shrugged and continued his banter.

As the sun slowly set, the birds were no longer in sight. The four riders entered the village of Eleb. A few of the small homes had yellow light coming from the oiled cloth windows. A Rarfell guard saw the riders and stopped them. Apparently recognizing Lerah and Darrca, the man immediately ran into a building. Urith noticed a cask top mounted by the door, which showed it was a tavern. Soon, more of the guards streamed from the building. They lined up for the queen, who nodded her appreciation. She pulled her long hair back over her shoulders while sitting proudly in the saddle as she passed them. Even after the hard day of travel, Darrca looked radiant in the glow of the dusky evening.

As Urith looked around the village, he didn't see any villagers looking out from their doors. The quiet hush over the streets seemed strange for the kingdom's ruler. As he passed the first few Rarfell warriors, the warrior paid little attention to them. Until he saw the next guard's tunic. A large dark stain along one side showed despite the dim light. Then Urith noticed the man's stance, trying to hide the stain. He moved his mount closer to Yartha.

"Something's wrong here," he whispered.

"What are you talking about?" the Gallaeci glanced over.

Urith turned his head to inspect the line of Rarfell Guards closer. He heard the stretching sound of leather from Yartha's saddle as the man turned toward Urith. The Esterblud didn't notice his companion swing his arm. But the warrior felt the blow to his head, then the sensation of falling before he hit the ground.

~~~

Urith stumbled along with a massive headache. His hands bound by a leather strap that extended to the ossane in front of him, the warrior struggled to keep up with the pace of the caravan. The line of mounted Borrs moved through the narrow confines along a sheer cliff face Urith remembered from the day before. Lerah led the column, followed by Darra, who kept her proud bearing despite her dirty and ripped clothing. Yartha followed the queen, his attention on her bare shoulders. He looked back occasionally at the Esterblud.

Urith felt the breath of the ossane behind him. He glanced back to see the Borr rider, still dressed in a Rarfell Guard tunic, give him a deadly grin as the man pushed his mount into Urith. Standing so close, Urith recognized his black helmet hooked to the Borr's saddle as a trophy. On the edge of the long drop to the bottom of the crevice, the Esterblud kept leaning against the long neck of the ossane to keep from falling over the side. One more mounted ossane brought up the rear of the column. Urith guessed the rest of the bandits remained behind to ensure control of Eleb.

As Urith stumbled along, he looked over his wounds the best he could as he stumbled along. His head wound no longer bled, but he felt the dried blood flaking off the side of his face. As the ossane pushed into him, Urith felt a prick in
~~~

his forearm. He looked down to see a spare spear tip remained lodged in his belt. He suppressed a grin, glad that the bandits missed it.

"You're wondering why you still live, Esterblud?" Yartha's sudden question caused Urith to lower his wrists as he glared.

"Not really, just thinking of how I'm going to get my revenge!"

The bandit laughed. He placed his hand on the Clovel Sword that he now carried on his waist belt. Urith's shield hung on Yartha's ossane as a trophy. Bitterness filled the Esterblud at the sight.

"That's not part of the Heptarc Code. Perhaps your walk to Cymeer will change your mind?"

"The code is malleable and twisted to suit a warrior's pleasure. Killing you will please me!" Urith continued, rubbing his leather binding against the spear tip in his baudrik belt.

"Oh, you don't like me now. I picked you out at the tavern because I knew your name. Phillo put me into Cymeer for the last two seasons. I wasn't worried about those men Reach and Hera gathered for their guard. But I saw you pass by with one of our men you captured. I had a suspicion you were worthy of standing before Phillo."

"I see you don't proudly wear the tattoos of the followers," the Esterblud growled. "They were easy to spot and kill."

"Yes, some of us carry our symbols on our chest so we can walk among our enemies."

Urith remained quiet, content to let the man talk.

"You feel betrayed. I don't know why you should. A few drinks between men never reveal a man's true intentions. Yet, you survive because I told the men not to kill you. Aren't you interested in knowing more about the cause you were supposed to stop?"

"Only if it will shut you up!"

Yartha snorted.

"You will soon meet our great leader, Phillo. He is a direct offspring of Facarm. His battle skills are unrivaled." He looked back at Urith. "Phillo was trained by the great Ecirr, son of Ecarca. Soon, he'll build an empire to rival the demigods of the past."

Urith looked up at the rider. He knew the names. The skalds song of the demigod Facarm who was the son of Camulas, one of the old gods. Facarm carried a bloody reputation which involved hunting humans. He also conquered the lands of Esterblud before the great Esterblud king, Uwal, finally killed him. The Gallaeci worshipped the Facarm since his death. It was the first Urith heard Ecirr remained alive.

"All the Gallaeci claim to descend from Facarm," the Esterblud scoffed. "I've heard tales about Ecirr and the band of demi-gods who call themselves the Huntsmen. Strangely, these Huntsmen never come near a well-armed kingdom. A man can claim anything."

"You remain skeptical, but you saw how the Borrs follow Phillo to their death. I was like you once. Phillo's men raided my village when I was a child. They killed my family, and I waited for my death. As I stood next to my father's body, I met the leader of the Gallaeci. I fell to my knees, expecting my death. Instead, Phillo lifted me from the ground. He explained that I'm the blood of Gallaeci, therefore an offspring of Facarm. He told me about my future in his world. It was the Huntsmen who told him to rule required the use of their methods. At each village, they wipe the slate clean and the strongest become followers. It was my option. I would stay with them and learn their ways. Otherwise, they banish those who don't accept this judgement into the mountains to depend upon the Fates."

"Too bad you didn't have the nerve to accept banishment," Urith growled.

Yartha glared at him, then grinned.

"Still too stubborn to accept your destiny. I remember my father's advice. Never depend upon the Fates! That is why I carry the mallet like Phillo."

Urith glanced back at the bandit near him. The man appeared half-sleep in his saddle. The Esterblud kept his bound wrists low while using the ossane next to him to keep Yartha from noticing his sawing against his belt.

"After our fight, I knew you were worthy to meet Phillo," Yartha continued to talk. "I believe you'll see his wisdom and why all the Gallaeci clan must join the cause. As you know, the Borrs are just another band of Gallaeci before Phillo. Now they grow strong with the help of people like me. My clan is now part of the Borrs' leadership. Soon, more will join us."

"I'm not of your tribe. In fact, my lineage killed Facarm. We Esterbluds take pride in that," Urith happily reminded him.

"That's true. However, Phillo wants excellent warriors. Your bloodline and Heptarc Code cannot stand against our beliefs. There is no need for gods when you follow the way of Facarm. I'll lead you to a life of a true warrior. A life of drink, food, and slaves to satisfy your needs."

"You delude yourself," Urith shot back, nearly falling over the road edge when the ossane next to him pushed him dangerously close to the side of the road.

Yartha smiled when he saw Urith's struggle to keep on the road. "Do I? I see the irony in your predicament. You told me how willing you are to die in battle. It is the premise of your life. You wish to die in battle, or your spirit cannot get to Haligulf. Yet, if you fall down that ravine, you wonder about the world as the Fates decide."

The Gallaeci slowed his mount, causing Urith to look at him.

"Am I wrong about your dilemma?" Yartha's firm belief in Phillo's ideas was clear as he pushed to persuade Urith.

"Tell me, didn't I describe the life of Haligulf for those who follow Facarm? Why would you wait to die in a vain hope of an afterlife? You can have such a life here. I've seen you fight, and I know of your honor. What I offer is a fighting life with the riches of drink, food, and slaves. Stay and fight with us or depend upon the Fates."

Urith remained stone faced at the thought. Yartha frowned.

"I see. You are too stubborn to consider the truth, even when it's handed to you. Well, my friend, Phillo, doesn't offer banishment as an option to a warrior when you reject the choice."

"Meaning he'll have something else in store for prisoners," Urith suggested. He felt the bindings on his wrists loosen as Yartha nodded.

"If you decide the wrong path, then you'll face the trail by horuks. Phillo uses them to determine your fate."

"Again, not likely," Urith growled as he stopped. The leather strap holding his wrists to Yartha's mount broke away. The Esterblud suddenly reached up and grabbed the Borr rider who let his ossane come next to Urith. He yanked on the surprised man's leather armor, trying to dismount the rider. His action caused the ossane to rear back.

As the Borr yelled out, Urith felt the road fall away as his feet suddenly dangled over the stone edge. His shifting weight forced the ossane to stumble and Urith could only hang on. The panicked mount's frantic snorting increased as the loose dirt gave way. Sliding over the side of the cliff, the animal's screams mixed with yells from the Borr rider and Urith. The mix of animal and humans tumbled over an outcropping as their momentum picked up, kicking up dust and dirt into the air.

Urith kicked away in desperation from the screaming ossane while one of the cloven hoofs struck him in the leg. Dropping away, his body slammed into a narrow line of bushes, which slowed his progress downward. However, the vegetation redirected his path and Urith slid behind the rider and his ossane.

When the trio finally reached the bottom, the rider landed on his mount. Urith slid into the animal as well. The stunned Borr tried to grab his sword, but the Esterblud used his momentum to land on his enemy's back. He quickly laced his fingers together around the Borr's forehead. With his knee between the man's shoulder blades, Urith wrenched back. He heard the snap of the Borr's neck over the dying cries of the ossane. Breathing heavily, the Esterblud slide away from the body.

On the trail above, the column of remaining riders saw dust wafting in the still air along the path of the long plunge. Pieces of the rock face continued to tumble down after the ossane finally went quiet. From their vantage point, Lerah and the others waited until their obscured view finally cleared enough to see the outcropping, but nothing below.

"They're dead!" Lerah concluded.

"Someone should make sure." Yartha looked along the edge of the trail.

"There's no way down there without ropes." Then the Gallaeci smiled. "Even if one of them lived, no one is getting out of that crevice alive."

"Come on," Lerah spurred his ossane. "We need to get back to Cymeer. We have people waiting for us."

Darrca continued to look down at the place where she watched Urith slide into oblivion.

"My queen, please continue on. Phillo waits for you." Yartha smirked as he pushed his ossane forward into hers.

"As your brother explained last night, we can't keep him waiting for his next bride. You'll soon meet your competition."

Darrca shot a deadly glance at Yartha. The man grinned, then blew a kiss at her. She spurred her ossane, and he laughed as he quickly caught up with her. Lerah slowed his mount, forcing the woman to slow after witnessing their exchange.

"Gallaeci, don't expect that you'll get away with such insults to a queen of Rarfell when we return to Cymeer. I swear Phillo will hear of this." Lerah insisted.

"What makes you think he'll care?" Yartha scoffed. "You don't understand what's in store for you and your sister."

Lerah started to reply, but decided against the idea. Instead, he pushed his ossane to speed up. Darrca spurred her mount as well as she took one last glance back.

At the top of the ridge, the road widened enough for the queen to pass her brother. When she tried, he grabbed her reins.

"You're no longer in charge, so don't forget that, Darrca. The arrangement will place me as Regent over Rarfell. My alliance with Phillo and the Borrs is inevitable. With the destruction of the remaining Rarfell Guard in Eleb, you have no one to support your claim."

"You betrayed your king and your tribe. I can no longer call you brother." Her voice quivered with rage.

Lerah frowned. "You forget that had you chosen your brother over your weak husband, none of this was necessary."

"Had these bandits not taken my dagger, I'd plunge it into your worthless heart."

She spurred her mount in frustration, still unable to move past Lerah.

From behind them, Yartha broke out in laughter. He glanced back at the Borr fighter behind them.

"Take the lead, so these two quit their squabbling," Yartha ordered. As the man passed him, the Gallaeci turned back to the brother and sister.

"When we get to Cymeer, I'm tempted to give Darrca her dagger back. Lerah, I don't think you would last long in a fight with your sister."

~~~

Not long after the column of riders left, Urith finished wrapping a length of cloth around his calf to staunch the bleeding. It was a painful wound caused by the sharp flint rocks scattered along the area. Although he couldn't see the trail above, he heard their voices echoing down. Not close enough to make sense of their words, he waited. When he heard the rhythmic sound of hoofs fade away, Urith lifted himself from his meager hiding place between two thin wstinga bushes. He limped over to the corpse of the Borr. The warrior picked up his black helmet. Partially mashed on one side by the ossane, he hooked his helmet to his belt. Then, Urith took the man's weapons along with the bags from the dead ossane. After throwing the bags over his shoulder, he
~~~

started limping along the bottom of the valley, hoping to find a trail back to the road before dark.

~~~

The following day, Lerah led the small group of riders past a patrol of a dozen Borrs just outside of Cymeer. The men on the patrol wore leather armor breastplates, and the captured helmets of the Rarfell Guards. The followers of Phillo refused to move off the road until they recognized Yartha and the Borr fighter who rode with them.

Forced to halt at the gates when a band of Borr guards stopped him, Lerah tried to pass. When the men refused to move for the man, Lerah started swearing at the guards. Clad in the captured tunics of the Rarfell Guards and carrying halberds, the Borrs grew angry and instantly surrounded the small band. They pointed the weapons at Lerah and the queen.

"Rarfell's Queen and her brother return for Phillo's judgement." Yartha called out as he pressed his ossane closer to the bearded leader of the guards. The man nodded and ordered his men to open a path.

"You can speak to Phillo about your treatment," Yartha smirked at Lerah while he spurred his mount past the man.

"That's not the agreement," Lerah growled out.

Yartha beamed at the comment.

"You can tell that to my overlord. In the meantime, you'll follow me to your quarters." The Gallaeci turned to the leader of the guards.

"Bring along a few of your men to guard our prisoners."

The Gallaeci took the reins of Darrca's ossane and led the queen into the town. He glanced back and saw the fury in the woman's eyes at his actions. However, she remained quiet while several of the Borr guards walked alongside her ossane.
~~~

When the barracks and Yartha stopped them at the open doors. Sliding off his mount, he ordered the brother and sister off their ossanes.

"Why are we going here?" Darrca stood there, looking at the dark interior.

"Come on," Yartha ignored her. "Your accommodations await."

The queen's initial reluctance brought a smile to the Gallaeci's face. One of the Borr fighters smacked the woman on the butt with the wooden shaft of his weapon. She turned around, cursing at him. The other guards laughed.

"I said, come on!" Yartha grabbed her shoulder. As he pulled the queen with him, the Gallaeci felt her hand on his belt. An instant later, Darrca held Yartha's dagger in her hand. The proud queen sliced at the shocked man, who was too slow in his retreat. Her blade sliced into his forearm.

Two of the Borr guards subdued Darrca while Lerah looked on the scene. He tried to pull the men away from his sister, only to get punched several times by a furious Yartha. Lerah fell to the floor next to Darrca.

After retrieving his dagger from a guard, he reached down and grabbed the queen by her robe. Hoisting the woman to her feet, Yartha placed the blade a next to her cheek.

"You're lucky that Phillo had his sights on you! I'd make it my duty to break you like a wild ossane," the Gallaeci fumed. He pushed her inside the building.

"Put them in the cells," he ordered the guards, sliding his dagger into his belt. As they forced the queen into the building, Yartha worked to staunch the bleeding with pressure. He hurried to his ossane.

"I hope they didn't kill the *mhoda*," he growled to himself. As he rode in the direction of the healer's house, the Gallaeci quietly vowed retaliation.

That docke does not know the things I'll do to her when Phillo leaves!

~~~

While the queen and her brother slept in the filthy cells inside the barracks, Urith finally spotted the dark tavern at the crossroads leading to either Ynyover or Cymeer. The twin moons of Kamin were only a quarter-full, making it difficult to see. His long journey by foot took much longer than he expected. Forced to walk near the road while keeping an eye out for bands of tattooed men, Urith took a quick nap right after sundown after avoiding a group of armed Borrs who now traveled wearing the tunics of the Rarfell Guards. Their tattooed faces made it easier to spot from a distance. After he rose from his sleep, the moonlight allowed him to follow the road. While his leg still hurt but his wound showed no signs of infection. Still, the injury caused him to limp.

His travel gave the young warrior time to think about the mistakes of King Renni. His advisors failed to account for the strength of Phillo's followers and their ability to meld with the people traveling and staying within Rarfell. Rech and Hera were overly confident that their small number of warriors would contain the Borrs. Like him, their overconfidence led to disaster. In hindsight, Urith overlooked too many questions which came to his mind about Yartha, as well as Lerah.

I must always remain suspicious about people!

Urith realized that Phillo's overthrow of Rarfell showed a great danger to his overlord back in Esterblud. He grappled with the best course of action. He considered returning to his homeland with the news of the Gallaeci. But to lose his
~~~

Clovel Sword brought terrible shame. A precious weapon from his famed encounter with a Clovel monster, the sword meant almost as much as his life. He must retrieve it. On top of that, he felt an obligation to the queen for his failure, not to mention Mekan and Dutra. Urith decided that retrieving his sword and taking down Phillo meant a greater chance at getting to Haligulf.

It was the honorable way!

As he took the final few paces to the quiet structure, Urith slowed. The ossanes outside remained tethered to the rail across the front. It was a sign that the people sleeping inside were leaving at first light. He came next to an ossane, whispering soothing words as he stroked the long neck of the animal. The saddles bore the mark of Rarfell Guards, which meant the men inside were Borrs. His anger grew with each quiet step he took toward the entrance.

Silently, Urith climbed the wooden stairs. As he remembered, the loft area held straw-filled beds laying in two rows on either side of the stairway. A single oil light burned low. However, it was enough to see the forms of three men who slept. The Esterblud slid out his captured short sword along with a dagger. As he reached the foot of the first bed, the floorboard creaked. In a flash, the fighter in the bed rolled on to the floor with a sword in hand. Despite the initial surprise, Urith quickly recovered to impale the man in the chest as he tried to rise from the floor. The clattering noise of the Borr's sword striking the floor woke the other two men.

As the closest man lifted himself from his bed, the Esterblud sprang over the top of the cot in his way. Urith's injured leg caused him to stumble, but he landed on the fighter. Both men went to the floor between the beds. Urith slid his dagger under his enemy's breastplate, his blade cutting into the flesh of his ribs. The Borr howled out as he elbowed the Esterblud in the jaw. However, the blow failed to stop Urith. He lifted his weapons and savagely plunged his dagger into the back of the man's neck. The body quivered beneath him as the warrior hurriedly pushed himself up from the floor.

The last Borr attempted to escape down the stairs. Urith grabbed the Clovel Sword and flung it in front of the escaping man. The long blade slid between his enemy's legs and tripped him. The bandit fell across the stairway and tumbled down steps. The man's sword clattered along the steps during his fall. Urith swiftly grabbed his sword and limped after him. Reaching the bottom while his enemy futility tried to defend himself, the warrior impaled the Borr in his belly with the short sword.

The backdoor of the tavern opened and yellow light from a lantern fell over the scene as the owner entered. The fat man watched with incredulity as the dying man gasped for help.

"Give Caruun my curse," Urith coldly stated as he twisted, then brutally pulled out the blade. The Borr's last scream filled the room.

Slowly, the tavern owner carefully drew closer, glancing between the Borr's open eyes and the big man standing over the body. Urith glanced over at the man holding the lantern. Then, he recognized the Esterblud.

"You can bury the bodies and keep their supplies. I'm taking their ossanes and swords."

"But these men have friends," the man stammered out. "Don't you know the Borrs control our land now? They patrol the roads. The Rarfell Guards no longer protect us."

"Then you better bury the bodies deep," Urith growled out. "I see the symbol of the Rarfell tribe on your mantel. Are you not from King Renni's clan?"

"We are Rarfell people," a large woman agreed as she entered the building. "You came through before with the big man who carried a hammer in his belt. He now returns to Cymeer after telling us this man called Phillo rules. But we're only tavern owners. We cannot fight against these Gallaeci."

Urith bent over the body and wiped the blood from his sword blade. He glanced up at the woman.

"What if I tell you that I saw Lerah, her brother, admit that he helped in the death of your king and clan leader? Now, Phillo and he will rule. Do you approve of a Cyer taking over? I doubt your elders will."

The news caused the woman to turn to her husband.

"The Esterblud is correct. Find men to help get these bodies out of here."

The fat man hesitated, then left them. Urith stood after cleaning his dagger, then slid the weapons into his belt. He looked down at the dead man's boots, then kneeled to retrieve them.

"At least this Borr was good for something. Pour dirt over the blood here," he recommended after he finished exchanging the footwear. "If the bandits ask questions, you can tell them these men went into the woods after me. I'll take their ossanes along that route to give you cover."

"I'll inform our people of Lerah and that cursed queen's treachery." The woman said as she went to the body.

"Darrca had nothing to do with it. She'll lead your kingdom well if given a chance. I believe Phillo wants her to ensure his rule with your elders. Marriage at sword point awaits her. Make sure you spread the truth."

Urith went to the door. "I saw bows and arrows for use by those who rise to fit on the side of Rarfell. Bring their swords to me. I may have use for the swords."

"What is one man to do?" The woman bent over the body, pulling the dead man's leather bag from his belt. "You cannot take on the Borrs alone."

The Esterblud paused, then looked back with a sneer grin on his face.

"That's true, I suppose, but I'm only going after three men."

Chapter 4: Delivery to the Fates

The morning light crept across the sky as the noise of her cell door opening woke Darrca. The massive bulk of Phillo squeezed past the narrow doorway. He had an oil lamp in his hand which revealed the man's muscular arm. Cold brown eyes stared at the queen, then order his men to bring her as turned away. Two guards swiftly entered and forced the queen to her feet.

They held the woman by her arms and followed Phillo. The group left the barracks and went across the grounds. After they passed the fence being constructed in the middle of the field, Darrca saw a line of dead hanging by their ankles from the balcony of her home. The disfigured and naked bodies of men, women, and children slowly twirled at the ends of the ropes. Spears stuck in the ground held the heads of some of the dead. She hardly recognized her husband's head as she passed by. The queen stopped in her tracks at the sight.

"How dare you treat a king like that!" she screamed.

Phillo glanced back, surprised at her reaction, before he continued walking.

"You'll hang next to him if you don't come along."

Darrca felt a hand on her back as one guard pushed her forward. She avoided looking at the body. The queen focused on her memories of her husband and the good times they shared. Occasionally, Renni broke from his busy schedule and they would talk by the light of the fire. In her heart, she knew her husband was more priest than king. He understood much about the history of their kingdom. In their occasional discussions, her husband enjoyed listening to Darrca's thoughts about issues as she saw them.

A Borr fighter, clothed in a Rarfell tunic, stood at the entrance when they arrived. He held open the door for Phillo. When the queen entered her home, she heard a pitiful groan. A bloodied Rarfell Guard hung by his thumbs from the banister with his bare foot just off the floor. After another look, she recognized the man who tried to save her and the king.

It was Hera!

The bound man's head lolled over when he heard the group climbing the stairs. His swollen eyes barely opened, and he caught sight of Darrca behind Phillo. The Rarfell Guard leader dropped his head in anguish at his failure.

The group stopped inside the king's bedchambers. Phillo ordered the guards to leave, then stepped to a table. Four women in white robes bowed as he took berries from a bowl.

"These are my other wives," the man mumbled out, then wiped red juice from his lips with his arm.

Darrca backed away as the women encircled her. Their expressions held no sympathy for the woman. The queen couldn't understand their open hostility to her presence. However, she recognized some necklaces and ornaments which revealed the wives' clan ties. Two were obviously pregnant, their bellies extending past the folds of their robes.

"Tomorrow, we'll go before your people and you will tell them you will marry me. You wish to avoid the unnecessary deaths of Cyer and Rarfell people. This will ensure the lasting partnership of your tribe and the Gallaeci." Phillo walked over to the window. He pushed back a decorated blanket, then opened the shuttered panels.

"There are some who might oppose the idea, but my men will see to their deaths."

"What makes you think that I'll do this?" Darrca lashed back. "I'm a Cyer queen who rules this land. I don't abide by my traitorous brother's plans."

He glanced back.

"Bring her!"

The women forced Darrca to the window.

"In those cages, you will find my favorite pets." He put his muscular arm around her shoulders. "Take a good look at them."

The queen looked down at the two horuks. The large flightless birds with dark black feathers stood about as tall as the man next to her. Their gray hooked beaks pecked at the bars on their cage while they stumped back and forth on their sharp talons. One cocked its head to eye the people looking down from the window.

"They're quite rare and seldom seen. The horuks hunt in groups," Phillo stated. "When we place our prisoners in the pen, the two birds stalk one victim, which they cull from a group of humans. Then they strike at their meal with their beaks and talons. Their victim grows weak from the bleeding and eventually will fall. Once their prey lies on the ground, the horuks will gut them alive. They've learned to feast upon the liver first. I've found these creatures are brutal yet fair when we leave the group of captives with them. They'll only kill one prisoner per day. So, a person's living or die depends upon the Fates for that day."

He patted the woman on the shoulder and smiled at her obvious fear.

"If you don't agree to my terms, then I'll declare that you and your brother betrayed King Renni. Rumors to that effect are already spreading in your kingdom, thanks to my men. Depending upon how long I decide to let you live, you will know nothing but pain and humiliation, as my men will publicly rape you for your betrayal. After that, the horuks get you. Just think, once these creatures dispose of your body, no one will remember Queen Darrca."

Phillo turned from the window, leaving the woman to stare at the creatures.

"I suggest you don't refuse my kind offer."

Phillo took more berries from the table. "What is your answer?"

He shrugged when Darrca remained quiet. The Gallaeci leader went toward the door.

"Exactly what do you want of me?" Her voice broke.

"Just as I stated earlier. You will publicly agree to marriage with a smile. I realize you are breaking with custom by this, but you may express the need to heal the kingdom. Either way, the people have little choice. I'll be their new overlord and you will continue as queen."

As he continued eating, his eyes assessed her.

"As you can surmise, I've planned this for quite a while. I've already had my men bring in the elders of your tribes to watch the ceremony. My men ensure that any hesitancy by anyone to my plan brings instant death."

Phillo went back to the queen. Her head bowed, she barely nodded.

"What is your answer? A true queen will look me in the eye and tell me plainly," he uttered ominously.

Darrca's moist eyes glared at him. "I accept your terms, but don't expect me to like them."

Phillo laughed and patted her head. She swatted his arm away.

"There's a good pet. Now, my wives will bath and prepare you. I advise you to listen to them, for they are survivors of my judgement. Each carries their own desires to live and survive in my harem."

The man walked to the door.

"Don't worry, my dear; tomorrow's marriage is nothing but a formality. All women captured by the Borrs become wives or they die. Because you're a noble woman, you'll bear me sons to extend my reign across the lands. It's only natural for you to bear the children of a demi-god."

As the man closed the door, his wives descended on their new competitor.

While Phillo ate with his advisors, Lerah came before him. As the brother of the queen entered the room below the stairs, he heard his sister's screams amid raucous laughter.

"What are you doing to Darrca?"

"Your sister is not cooperating with my wives," Phillo leaned back in the elaborate chair of the king. "I believe in competition. My wives wish to remain on top or I might give them to the horuks. Like all prisoners, Darrca will learn that her new role is serving me and my other wives. Two of my wives enjoy a woman as much as I do. Your sister will learn quickly."

Lerah frowned as he glanced at the stairs where more laughter broke out along with the noise of a strap smacking bare skin. A pitiful, muffled cry of pain came into the room.

"Phillo, we made an agreement. There's no reason to treat me or her as your enemy. I'm to be Regent over Rarfell after my sister marries you. I can control her."

The massive man at the table glared at Lerah, who feared he had overstepped.

"You can't control an ossane without help," he scoffed. "You must never forget that my enemies die by my hand. For the moment, you are not my enemy." The Borr leader took another bite before returning to the conversation.

"You still have a value for me. As long as Darrca remains compliant to our plans, I'll ensure that you're named Regency. I need this façade to placate the elders. I don't want to kill everyone in this land. We need peasants to till the soil and become servants now that my people fill Rarfell."

The men around the table laughed. Phillo watched Lerah's eyes narrow at the idea. However, the man accepted his direction.

"Just as we agreed. I promise my sister will follow you. She is weak and unable to think about the future. You do not need to worry about my loyalty," the traitor replied.

"You remind me of a *feorag* hunting for nuts," Phillo scuffed. "Of course, I have no worries about you. If your sister fails, then she dies, and I'll have you flayed alive for the betrayal of King Renni. That will placate the elders of Rarfell."

He pointed to Lerah's guard.

"Put him back in the cell so he remembers my words. Tomorrow, Lerah shall be my guest at the ceremony. Also, have men take down my trophy that hangs by his thumbs on the stairway. We'll use him to feed my horuks in the morning. It's a fitting wedding gift for my wife."

As the guard pushed their reluctant visitor from the room, the men at the table continued their meal.

"Why bother letting Lerah stay alive? He barely knows how to pick up a spear." Yartha sat a clay pitcher of heathmead next to Aralla. The old Gallaeci fighter carried a savage-looking scar over his left eye socket and Yartha knew the general of the Borrs couldn't see the pitcher from the angle. Phillo recognized the perpetual jokester's intent, and he pointed to the heathmead. With a frown, Yartha moved it into Aralla's line of sight.

"You still act as the boy I recall," Phillo snorted. "To answer your question, everyone knows Lerah's weak. He is useful as a person who speaks to elders of the Cyer tribe. Should they grow weary of him, then they'll cut his throat. Are we now in full control of Rarfell?

"Yes, with the fall of Eleb, we control every town," Sarcam spoke up with food still in his mouth. "Our plan went even better than I expected. King Renni followed Lerah's advice about splitting his warriors into smaller groups to defend all the small hamlets. Putting our Rarfell allies into those villages was the master stroke. The Rarfell Guard did not know what happened until we hung them." He almost smiled.

"I had the mear of Telsa nailed to a tree to die of exposure and any person wearing the Rarfell colors and carrying weapons we hung. It will reinforce your will. However, we need a replacement for the leader of the village. Eventually, some of our Gallaeci clan people will fill these roles, but we remain limited in numbers. For the moment, we must rely on our Rarfell allies until our people bring their families here."

"Yes, we'll transform Rarfell soon," Phillo slapped the tabletop.

"The mear from Eleb is gone as well. My men already took the village, and we used him as a target," Yartha leaned back in his chair, holding his drink. He looked down at his bandaged arm. "Unfortunately, Darrca wasn't willing to use her dagger skills to end the man's suffering. She's not strong, really only suitable for bedding."

"Perhaps you have ideas of what you want to do with Darrca? I heard she used a knife on you." The Gallaeci leader leaned forward and ripped off a large piece of erba meat from a platter. He saw Yartha's eyes narrow at the slight, but the man remained quiet.

"My young friend, you don't need to worry about the queen. She doesn't strike me as one who will last long within our society. You did well as my primary spy inside Cymeer. Perhaps you should become the mear for Eleb. Is this something you wish for?" Phillo stuffed his mouth.

"No, I'm better suited for leading Cymeer." Yartha stated. He noticed Phillo raise his eyebrows at the idea.

"I know every person and place in this town," he continued to explain. "I even had one of our fighters ensure that a farm girl I like remains in the house of Rech? She's suitable for my needs."

The young Gallaeci smiled deviously and Phillo nodded.

"Sarcam, it appears my young protégé learns quickly. Perhaps we should keep a closer eye on Yartha. You don't trust him." Phillo turned to the broad, short man whose dark complexion and death-like expression unsettled many Gallaeci.

"Skalds told me of a great general who once placed his best lieutenants in charge of captured territory. But they always placed those men in a way to force them to watch each other. You can achieve the greater goals when a replacement waits in the wings."

"Facarm was a genius!" Phillo smiled as he recalled the verse of Gallaeci tales. "I find your suggestion well thought out."

"As we discussed before, Rarfell is the base to build my army to invade the lands of Ynyover. I'll send word to all Gallaeci. They are welcome here." Phillo smiled at his plan.

"Sarcam, you go to Eleb as the new mear."

The dark man, who never smiled, simply nodded.

"Then, you will bring in more Gallaeci to Eleb and begin the push of our tribe into the isolated parts of Cahmais. This can help hide our strategy from merchant travelers," Phillo explained. "In the meantime, Aralla will train our forces as we expand the number of warriors who align with us."

Sarcam glanced over at Yartha, then he nodded. Phillo held up his mug of heathmead.

"Very well, Yartha, you have Cymeer. We need more warriors. That's your focus. As I told you before. Your men will find candidates worthy to follow Facarm. Send those fighters to Sarcam and he will train them. Otherwise, you ensure Lerah controls the elders of the tribes. If not, eliminate him. Do you understand?"

Yartha raised his drink as well. "I look forward to it."

"Good, then I'll placate the king of Cahmais. I'll send a messenger wearing Rarfell colors to him to ensure he doesn't interfere with our plans. Neither Cahmais nor Esterblud can intercede into Ynyover without breaking their treaty. As I've always said, Rarfell provides us with a great opportunity."

Phillo finished his drink. He looked at the ceiling. It was mostly quiet now. The sounds drifting into the room came from the women who whispered orders, followed by moans of passion. The man rose from the table.

"I believe my wives convinced Queen Darrca of her extra responsibilities. I'll join them."

~~~

Not long after sunrise, Urith arrived on the outskirts of the thin forest, which revealed Cymeer's walls. After dismounting from his ossane, he tied the animal out of sight along with the others that he took from the Borrs. Retrieving a bag of water along with another that carried his food, the Esterblud crept to a shaded place. Hidden in the shadows and
~~~

leaves, the place allowed him to view the movement of people entering and leaving from the main gate. He was far enough away from the closest farm to avoid their scrutiny as well.

His ride through the forest during the night progress slowly under the moonlight. The warrior took his time to travel upstream for a while to throw off any searchers of the missing the Borrs' fighters. Urith hoped he could keep them at bay until he found a way into the fortress undetected. At one point, he thought of stopping back at the farm where Mekan lived. However, he decided against the idea when he remembered how close to the main road where her farm was.

His head bobbed as he tried to shake off the lack of sleep while he leaned against the flaking bark of a *riate* tree. Urith pulled a piece of the bark that scribes made into a cheap parchment. He rolled it across his leg as he yawned. Fearing sleep would overtake him, the warrior carefully stood, trying to avoid a shot of pain from his leg injury. Staying in the shadows, he scanned the quiet area.

Two guards stood at the gate and none appeared along the battlements. The Borr's control of Rarfell appeared complete, and they feared no uprising from the population. The situation surprised him.

In Esterblud, three dominant tribes constantly jockeyed for power, leaving King Penhda spending much of his time on developing alliances and arranging marriages. Balancing the interest and fortunes among the clans required a delicate, yet forceful blend of leadership and planning. Urith witnessed little of that in Rarfell in his short time there. While Darrca appeared capable, she would never have a chance with her brother and Phillo.

As the Urith looked over gaps in the town's wall which he intended to exploit in the night. A wagon parked by a low section of the wall provided him an opportunity if it remained after dark. The warrior sat down and leaned against the tree again.

As he thought about his next steps, Urith decided he needed a robe to cover his chain mail. Urith worked on his beat-up helmet as he eagerly expected a showdown with Yartha. Still, he needed to determine what allies remained alive inside the town. His first aim was the barracks, where he hoped some of the Rarfell warriors remained alive.

Again, the need for sleep fell over him. He pulled the cork from his water bag and took a drink. He poured the water on his face.

It's going to be a long day!

~~~

Yartha entered the former home of Rech, where he found Mekan on her hands and knees near the front door. He dismissed the Borr guard, who watched over the woman scrubbing the bloodstains from the wood floor with a pumice stone. Next to the door, a roughhewn table now stood with a burning lamp. Drawn on the wall by the lamp was a crude-looking serpent wrapped around a mallet.

Yartha leaned against the wall as Mekan worked. After the guard left, the Gallaeci smiled as he knew the woman tried to ignore his presence.

"You've been given to me by Phillo. I'm now the mear of Cymeer."

Mekan's back-and-forth motion slowed, then increased as she continued scrubbing the floor.

"Get up from your knees, my pet. You can stop such menial work now."

She rose, focusing her gaze on the floor.
~~~

"Look at the symbol of the Borrs," he told her. "From now on, you'll ensure the oil lamp never stops burning." Yartha frowned when she refused to look at his shrine.

"I guess you'll learn to appreciate our beliefs soon enough. Fortunately, you're moving up in the world, Mekan. Like Darrca for Phillo, you'll be my wife. Now, put down that stone. The wife of a mear doesn't scrub the floors."

She dropped the stone, refusing to react as he came next to her. "You'll be able to bring one of the village women as your servant." He started playing with her hair. "You really should let your hair down."

Mekan tried to back away, and he grabbed her.

"I follow the teachings of Facarm who stated a man must have many wives to ensure a strong family line. You're the first."

"I won't be yours," Mekan told him as she jerked away from his grip. Yartha's smiled turned to a grim line.

"It's not your choice!"

He gave her a fake smile. "Don't worry, I'll treat you fairly. I'm not in a hurry for more wives. Did you know your queen is now the fifth woman that Phillo calls wife? He breeds the noble women of each tribe we overtake to extend his control over the lands he conquers."

Mekan stared at him.

"I despise you. I'll never marry you."

Yartha slapped her with the back of his hand, sending Mekan to the floor. When she looked back at him, her lip was bleeding.

"It's not your choice," he repeated. "Neither of us are of noble blood, so you suit my needs." He came closer.

"Do you think I've forgotten the wound in my leg that came from you? You'll pay me back with children."

"I'd rather die!" She held up her chin, waiting for him to strike. The blow sent her back.

"No, you won't die. Instead, I'll break you." He wrapped his arms around her. Mekan struggled as he tightened his grip, lifting her.

"I watched you, then overheard you with that Esterblud. You'll soon do the same with me." Yartha laughed. "Come now, you didn't think that an Esterblud cared about you? Like all nobles, they take the women they want. Besides, he'll never return for you. Should I tell you how he died? He screamed like the ossane he was on as they fell off the cliff."

Mekan stopped struggling and her head dropped at the news.

"However you live. That's why you're here with me. The conqueror takes the spoils of war, my little farm girl." Yartha sniffed her hair and loosened his grip. His hand caressed her shoulder. "Your moans and groans reached me as I lay upstairs in the tavern at night. That's why I know that you'll make me a good wife. Come now and show me your skills."

He tried to lead her to the stairs, but she refused to move. Yartha slid in front of her. Her determined expression made the large man shake his head slowly. He struck her again. Mekan fell to the floor in front of the stairs.

"I can do anything I want with you. For now, you'll bed with me like a docke." he grabbed her by her hair. "Now get upstairs before I get angry."

Slowly, the woman did as she was told. Tears fell down her cheeks, but she refused to move faster. The Gallaeci watched her.

"I'll break you soon enough. Then you'll realize the benefits of my friendship."

~~~
~~~

Night finally fell over the town of Cymeer. Urith watched the gates close as the sun set and waited until he saw no movement. Putting his helmet on for his expected battle, the Esterblud cautiously walked across the field. The starlight night gave scant light in the darkness. Every sound forced him to pause before he moved on. Finally, he reached the wagon he noticed earlier. The dim outline of the ragged ramparts above the wooden wall extended beyond his reach. However, the Esterblud came prepared. He swung the end of a looped rope over the sharpened tips of the log tops. A short time later, Urith climbed over the wall. He crouched on the walkway which he immediately recognized was overlooking the ossane pen. The stink made him wrinkle his nose. There was no movement below Urith, but he heard the grunts and neighing coming from below as the ossanes settled in for sleep. The lanterns strung along the walkway for the guards showed him no one was in sight.

Sliding down into the ossane pen, the warrior used the darker shadows along the edge of the wall to reach the trader's shack. Urith pressed his ear close to the open window, but he heard nothing. He carefully entered the building. Pulling a set of *tribolrocks* from his waistbelt, he placed the pair of rocks together. After a moment, the crystals from the mines of Neewar gave off a green glow. After a quick search of the room, he found a brown robe that smelled like the ossanes. He pulled on the clothing, which was too small for his frame. Urith compensated by ripping open the sleeves, then pulled the hood over his helmet. The warrior silently left the building.

Urith continued along the back of the building, using his hands to work his way between the buildings in the pitch black. The Esterblud stopped when he reached the front of a building at the end of the row. Across the narrow street, he watched two men in a mix of Rarfell colors and Borr leather armor as they played with a woman between them. The laughter among them along the yellow belt around the woman's waist showed her profession as a *docke* who pleased men for koinons. After they entered the tavern, Urith casually stepped across the street. He went by the front entrance, keeping his head down. The warrior reached the dark alley between the tavern and a merchant house. He slowly felt his way along, remembering the turns which led him to the alley across the road from the barracks. The light of oil lamps displayed most of the stone building. A Borr guard paced in front of the entrance. His bow hung over the shoulder and he carried a quiver of arrows.

He's an easy kill!

Urith considered killing the archer, but resisted the temptation. Another guard might come by to take over and sound an alarm. After waiting for the man to pass, Urith walked to the corner of the building. Keeping in the shadows, the Esterblud worked his way close to the entrance. The wood and iron door stood partially open. The Borr yawned, then walked away into the shadows. Before long, Urith heard the man urinating. After a quick glance around, he hurried through the open doorway and pulled to a stop in the shadowed corner. The quiet passage had a single oil lamp burning at the other end.

Urith remembered the Borr prisoners came from one side of the building. He headed toward the spot, hoping to find captured Rarfell guards. The Esterblud carefully walked along the hall as he looked for the cells. Turning a corner, he stepped into a narrow hall where a lamp burned. He almost ran into a man sitting on a bench. The half-asleep guard jumped up. As he yelled, Urith swung his sword. The Borr's head spun across the floor while his remains fell in a heap.

"Who's there? What are you doing?"

A voice startled Urith, and he swung around to see a row of iron bars along one wall. A bearded face peered out at him.

"Are you Rarfell?" Urith went to the cell.

"Yes, I'm Esart of the king's clan. My brother Parca is in the next cell." The man replied in a whisper. "Get us out of here and I'll give you everything I own!"

The Esterblud went to the body and pulled a large key from the dead man's belt. After opening the door, he gave the key to Esart.

"Get your brother and grab what weapons you can find." Urith went to the entrance to the main passageway.

After the two Rarfell men joined him, Urith turned to them.

"Are there others you can trust to join us?"

Esart shook his head.

"I don't think so. We're the only ones left who haven't died or given up and become part of the Borrs. The guard you killed told me we're to be sacrificed to the horuks in the morning."

"There's Hera!" Parca interjected. "I overheard a guard say they have him tied up outside. He was to join us in the horuk pen."

"Alright, lead the way and we'll get him." Urith paused when he looked at the farthest cell, which remained quiet. He thought he saw a face. Before he asked, the brothers took off around the corner into the main corridor. The Esterblud followed them to a door leading into another hall. Parca carefully entered, then waved them forward as he went to the side exit. The Rarfell opened the door and looked outside.

Urith followed the two men outside. The darkness made it difficult to see as they hurried away into the night.

As they drew closer to the king's residence, Esart stopped them. They ducked down by a fence when he pointed out two Borrs under a lantern by the stairs leading into the home. Looking around, Parca noticed a large pole recently put up near the pens. A person hung by his wrists on the pole.

"I think that's Hera," Parca whispered. "Let's go!"

The Rarfell took off while his brother and Urith hurried after him. After reaching the man hanging on the pole, the men hardly recognized the Cymeer Company leader. Hera's swollen face from the beatings caused his men to curse under their breath as they lifted him down. He groaned from the effort. Parca held him up.

"Quiet!" Urith hissed as he looked around.

He heard sounds in the pen. The Esterblud couldn't understand why they needed an ossane pen next to the overlord's palace. For a moment, he swore that a giant dark shadow moved inside. Stillness fell over them and he turned to the brothers.

"Hera's in no shape to help us. Two of us can go after those guards at the palace. Once we get inside, we can take down Phillo!"

"Are you *a brgensoc*? Only a crazy one tries to attack those men," Esart insisted. "You limp like an old man. It's open ground and the guards will see us before we get close enough. Even if we had an archer with us, one guard would probably signal an alarm. You'll get us killed or captured again!"

"Are you not willing to go to Haligulf?" The Esterblud growled.

The brothers glared at his insult.

"I can't see well," Hera suddenly whispered. "But that voice reminds me of that cursed Esterblud. Esart is right! I was in the king's home and you'll never get up the stairs. There are guards sleeping on the first floor." The man's strength gave out, and Hera dropped to his knees.

"Give me water!"

Urith cursed at the news.

"Alright, let's get out of here before someone sees us!" He reached down and picked up Hera. Urith put the man over his shoulder.

"Like an old man," the Esterblud muttered at Esart. Then he told the brothers to lead them to the ossane trader's sack.

Esart nodded, and he moved toward the shadows along the edge of the road. Urith followed, realizing the extra weight hurt his leg. After crossing to the dark buildings, Urith gave Esart his tribolrocks to help them through the dark alleys. He let Hera down and then he and Parca helped him through the dark streets.

It took several stops to avoid guards, but the group finally reached the trader's shack next to the city wall. After Urith laid Hera on the floor, Parca kneeled with a metal cup he grabbed by the ossane water trough. He put the metal cup to Hera's parched lips, and the man gulped down the liquid. Hera brought up his hands to hold the cup and Urith looked at the man's disfigured thumbs, painfully swollen. Parca went back out to the water trough outside for more.

"Hera, you're no good at fighting in that condition. The brothers can take you over the wall. There's a rope on the wall over there," Urith pointed as he took back his glowing rocks. He sat them on a bench, which gave the small shack a green glow.

"I have ossanes tied on the edge of the forest directly across from the wagon next to the town wall. Once you leave, I'll go back to find Phillo on my own."

"Urith, don't try it!" Hera coughed out. "Phillo isn't the only problem. I told you there are too many Borrs who'll kill you before you get close enough."

"I must get Darrca away," Urith looked out of the open window, lowering his voice. Seeing nothing, he turned back to Hera.

"Once I freed myself from Yartha, I thought of returning to Esterblud to find support from Penhda. However, I suspect the king will never send our warriors. It would bring war with Cahmais again. Phillo will divide and conquer your tribes by using Lerah as his loyal *calward* and the queen as a figurehead. That means I must act now!"

"You're being a fool. You can't get inside without fighting them, which will bring more," Hera took another drink, then continued. "Phillo hung me like I was his cursed trophy. I want him dead worse than you do. But he's given the buildings across the street from the palace to the Gallaeci, along with some of their families. Even some of the Cymeer Company joined Phillo. They planned this for at least a season, and they'll be on you before can get to Darrca."

"That means running away and leaving the queen to her fate!" Urith growled.

"That's already happened!" Hera told him bitterly. "These Borrs only accept power as their god. Phillo's wives whipped her into submission. I heard it happen. After the sun rises, they'll force Darrca to marriage in front of the elders of the tribes and all Cymeer. We cannot stop this with just the four of us."

"Curse the gods!" Esart exclaimed.

"Then you want to leave her?" Urith stood and savagely slammed the wall with his fist.

"What choice do we have? We must go into the countryside and gather more forces." Hera squinted at the Esterblud. "We can help gather those people we know will help us retake the other towns. Plus, we'll cut off supplies to Cymeer. The Borrs haven't enough warriors to cover all of our land."

"Esterblud, you are a worthy warrior, but this is not your fight." Hera insisted as he forced himself to sit up. "While I hung there, all I could think about was revenge. When I saw my queen pass by and accept her fate, I realized I must abandon her to save our lands from the Borrs."

Urith glanced down at the man.

"You're wrong! It is my fight. I've got two others waiting for help." He paused. "Wait, you said elders are here. Can't we find them to assist us? They must hear the truth."

"They already know. The Borrs killed any leaders who might oppose them. Anyone who remains in Cymeer is now loyal to Phillo or they give up their life. Now, you understand why we must gather men and return."

The Esterblud took a deep breath and sit on the bench. Urith pulled his hand through his hair. "You speak plainly, Hera. It doesn't go down well since I did not see my betrayal and the capture of your queen. Yet, I still have an obligation to others as well. Does anyone know what happened to Mekan or the boy, Dutra?"

A sound came from outside the shack, and the men grabbed their swords. Then, they heard a light knock on the door. It slowly opened and Dutra peered in.

"I heard my name!"

"What are you doing here?" Urith demanded.

Dutra stepped into the room with the same cocky grin on his face. His rags were gone. Instead, he wore a brown tunic and leather breeches. As he stepped inside, the sound of his boots caught Urith's attention. A long rip on one side of the tunic and the shoes told the Esterblud that Dutra must have stripped the clothes from one of the dead Borrs.

"I've been following you. You were easy to see when I heard you walking along the wall and coming this way. The guards seldom come this way. I sleep in this shack once the trader leaves. The Borrs didn't kill him." Dutra explained to Urith, then he looked down at Hera.

"Yartha took Mekan as his wife. He's the new mear for Cymeer."

"Not when I get through with him," Urith's deadly growl filled the room.

"I know how to get in and out of places without being seen," Dutra boasted. "I'll take you to the house where he stays now."

"It's not a smart plan. You should come with us," Esart told him.

"No, an Esterblud doesn't leave his sword with his enemy," the warrior rose and put one of his tribolrocks into the leather bag hanging from his belt. He handed it to Esart.

"I'll leave this for you to find your way back to the ossanes." He turned to Dutra.

"Dutra, take me to Yartha!"

After Urith left the building, Esart helped Hera to his feet.

"That Esterblud is going to have every Borr in Cymeer after him." Parca told them as he held open the door.

"Better him, than us." Esart stated.

Hera looked out into the darkness and thought of Mekan as both brothers helped him to Cymeer's walls. He didn't like the feeling of betrayal that swept over him.

I'll return to sweep the Borrs out of Rarfell!

~~~

Inside the dark room of the king's chambers, Darrca carefully slid out of the bed. She stepped around another bed where Hartcas slept. The oldest wife of Phillo still held the leather strap she used to beat the queen with. For a moment, Darrca considered strangling Hartcas with the strap. She even reached for the leather handle before changing her mind.

My duty is to my clan and kingdom! I'll have my revenge later.

Quietly moving to the window, the naked woman avoided the other beds where the other wives slept. She froze when she heard movement. Glancing at the bed where Phillo slept, fear nearly overwhelmed her. But the man's gigantic frame rolled over and he continued to sleep.

All I need is a knife to cut your calward off! I'll feed it to you the next time we meet!

Queen Darrca carried a savage vengeance in her heart against each person who violated her. Each time they raped her, she forced her mind to focus on the brutal ways she would have them killed. After a while, the thoughts allowed her to escape the demeaning ways they used her body. When they finished with her, the woman stared at each of them, imprinting their faces into her memory. Her tormentors would feel the queen's wrath until their dying breath. Once she escaped, the mountains would bleed rivers of Gallaeci blood.

Darrca quietly pushed opened a window shutter. No moonlight meant her chances of evading capture increased. When the woman looked down upon the field earlier that day, she recognized escape was her only possible chance to
~~~

survive. Darrca made careful observations of the main timbers and cross beams that showed on the outside wall. She recognized they provided a means to climb down.

Working her leg over the windowsill, she slid out onto the wall. The queen ignored the rough wood scraping the lashes and other wounds from her beating. Her foot slipped on the timber and she let out a grunt. Panic swept over her as she expected someone to wake. Holding her breath while hanging from the windowsill, Darrca heard nothing. Dangling for a moment until her foot caught the next beam, she then proceeded down the wall.

When she reached the ground, the woman felt her way along the building. When Darrca came around the corner, she immediately noticed a guard heading her way. She backed away, relieved the man had no lantern. The queen kneeled, shivering in the cool night air. As the sound of footsteps drew closer, she felt around the ground. Her hand came upon a rock. Lifting the heavy stone with both hands, she slowly stood. The guard came around the corner, his dark form barely seen in the shadow. It was enough for Darrca. She slammed the rock into the Borr's skull. The man hit the ground with a thump. She stood over him and slammed the stone on his head again. Warm blood splattered across her body. Darrca searched the body and found his dagger and sword which she sat next to her bare foot. Struggling to get the guard's robe off, the woman kept looking around. Finally, the cloth tore away. She threw on the clothing, disregarding the wet blood she felt on the tunic. Grabbing the stolen weapons, Darrca moved across the field. The stubble and rocks cut at her feet, but she ignored the pain.

The queen heard every sound, still expecting someone would raise an alarm. When she finally reached the wall,

Darrca looked back. Unsure of a good escape route, she realized the obstacle stood too tall for her to climb over. Darrca heard footsteps above her.

Guards!

She paused, waiting until the man walking along the platform above slowly moved away. She followed the wall in the opposite direction toward the ossane pen. Darrca's feet felt every bit of the rough path as she worked her way along. Finally, she reached the ossane pen. Trembling under the ripped robe, the queen tried to think of her options. Then, she saw a small person leave a tiny shack, followed by a large man limping behind him. Darrca drew closer when she heard talking inside the building. She expected them to be Borrs. However, as she drew closer, one voice sounded familiar. She went to the door as it opened. In the green glow of the tribolrock, she recognized one man.

"I truly hope this is not the last of my Rarfell guard," Queen Darrca told Hera, who stopped in his tracks at the sound of her voice.

~~~

When Urith entered the Rech's home with his battered battle helmet on and a sword in hand, he found an oil lamp burning on a table. The Esterblud expected someone remained awake. Then, he saw an image of a Gallaeci serpent recently drawn on the lime-covered wall.

I'll leave his bloody head on this cursed shrine!

Dutra stared wide-eyed at the picture as Urith carefully looked around. He glanced into the dark of the first room. As he moved toward the stairs, he noticed the shadow of his Clovel Sword and his battle shield hanging on the wall above him. Urith quickly climbed the stairs to retrieve his weapons. After the warrior pulled his shield from the wall, he put it on
~~~

his arm. When he reached for his Clovel Sword, he heard the squeak of a stair above him.

Yartha attacked, swinging his mallet down just as the warrior threw up his arm. The shield deflected the blow, but the force exposed Urith to the second weapon Yartha carried. He plunged his dagger into Urith's shoulder. The blade penetrated his chain mail, and the Esterblud yelled. Urith swung around with the edge of his shield, striking Yartha in the leg. The Gallaeci fell into Urith, his thick body knocked the warrior into the wall. Yartha flung out his mallet, striking Urith's helmet. The stunned warrior grabbed his opponent while trying to keep his balance.

In the dim light, neither fighter saw Mekan coming down the stairs behind the battle. She pulled the Clovel Sword from the wall. As the woman lifted the heavy weapon to strike, Yartha glanced back to see her. He swung back with his dagger, which cut her in the leg. Mekan dropped the Clovel Sword, grabbing her injured leg as the weapon noisily slid down the stairs. As Urith tried to grab it, Yartha came around and struck his enemy in the helmet with his mallet. It was a glancing blow that sent Urith tumbling down the stairs. The Esterblud landed heavily, sprawled across the wood floor.

Yartha reached the bottom of the stairs just as Urith tried to rise. The Gallaeci stomped his foot down on the warrior's shield arm. An anguished growl came from Urith with his elbow bent backward by the pressure of Yartha's weight.

"You die!"

The Gallaeci swung his mallet down on Urith's chest. Even with the chain mail and padded undergarment covering him, the blow forced the air from Urith's lungs. He heard the crack of ribs as waves of pain swept across his chest. All the

Esterblud could do was watch as Yartha lifted his weapon for the death blow.

Movement from behind the Gallaeci caught Urith's attention. Mekan came down the stairs and jumped on Yartha's back. Her attack sent them both flying across Urith's body. Mekan held on to the Gallaeci as they rolled across the floor, coming to a stop next to the entrance. Her arms wrapped around Yartha's neck; the woman savagely bit down. Her teeth cut through most of the man's ear as she tasted the blood. Yartha bellowed out in anger and pain.

Near them, Urith struggled to his feet, still unable to breathe. He felt Dutra next to him, struggling with the warrior's weight as Urith lifted an arm to hold on to the bannister. He watched the struggle, desperately trying to recover.

Yartha rolled over on Mekan, who kept her grip around his neck. Using his fists, the Gallaeci punched at the woman's head. Finally, he slammed his head back into Mekan's face. His blow broke the woman's nose and dazed her. Freed from her grip, Yartha rolled over and quickly rose to his feet.

While Mekan fought Yartha, Dutra retrieved the Clovel Sword from the floor. He forced it into Urith's hand as the Esterblud let go of the railing. He staggered over to meet Yartha, who swung his weapon. The crack of the metal on Urith's shield filled the entryway. The Esterblud pushed forward, sending his opponent back into the door while Mekan scrambled out of the way. As he raised his sword, the pain in his chest nearly forced Urith to his knees. He swung, but Yartha sidestepped the blade that sliced at the door. Urith slowly backed away.

Outside the door, everyone heard the yells of Borrs approaching. A smile came to Yartha's lips at the sound of help.

"You'll all die now!" He reached for the door handle.

Dutra grabbed the oil lamp that somehow remained lit amid the fighting. He threw the clay container at Yartha. It glanced off the Gallaeci, striking the door. The burning oil splattered across the man and the door. Yartha rushed away from the door, dropping his weapons and slapping at his back to stop the fire. The oil covered his hands and started spreading the fire. Now screaming, the Gallaeci fell to the floor, rolling around to knock out the fire.

"I'll finish him!"

Urith went toward his enemy when the burning door burst open. Flames spread along the wall as a Borr guard entered. Urith shoved his sword blade into the man's middle. However, he saw more fighters coming.

"Out the back," Mekan pulled on his arm.

Glancing at Yartha, Urith fought off the urge to go after him. He followed the woman and Dutra through the house. As they exited the building, the warrior glanced back to see the flames were already filling the room behind them.

Dutra took the lead, guiding the group through the dark alley. After reaching the next street, he asked where they were going.

"Get us back to the ossane stables," Urith told him. Taking a breath still hurt, but he pushed through. "We'll go over the wall and into the forest."

Durta hurried them across the street as they heard the cries and screams behind them. When they reached the alley next to a tavern, the boy stopped them. People with lanterns were hurrying into the alley. The trio hid in the shadows between two buildings until the villagers passed. As they rose from their hiding position, the group looked back to see light coming from flames rising from the thatched roofs.

"That's one way to escape!" Urith grunted.

The yellow light of the burning building allowed them to see more details as they crossed the road.

"I left a rope along the wall," the Esterblud whispered after they stopped in the shadows of a building. "Hera and his men should have left us an ossane." He pointed to the spot, nearly groaning from the pain in his chest.

"Hera's alive?" Mekan's pleased tone caught Urith's attention. A frown soon crossed her face.

"What happens when they come after us? We can't outrun ossanes." Mekan reminded Urith.

"I took the back way through the forest. We can keep to the thickest part, which will give us plenty of places to hide until we get out of Rarfell."

Even in the dim light, he saw her doubt while Durta nodded in agreement. Urith didn't wait for more discussion. He followed the path as he recalled his entrance route. When the Esterblud reached the wooden stairs, he quickly climbed to the top. As he stepped on top of the wooden platform, Urith found a Borr guard standing in his way. The surprised guard didn't have time to yell out. The warrior thrust his sword blade into the man's belly. As the Borr gasped, Urith rammed his shield into the guard's face. The Borr fell over the railing into the ossane pen below. Urith caught his breath with each movement of his chest, ripping a wave of agony through him. Durta stepped next to him.

"I'll become a warrior, if you'll teach me."

Urith glared at him briefly. After he carefully straightened, a sneer smile filled his face.

"Just remember that not every fight goes so easily!"

~~~

The next day, Phillo stood on his platform overlooking the crowd of Borr guards and villagers. Nearly everyone
~~~

looking up at their overlord remained covered in the soot and ash from fighting the fires. The remains of burned out shells still smoldered where a line of large homes once stood. After the people put out the fires, the leader of Cymeer had his guards gather around everyone in the village. Then, he received news about the escaped prisoners and the Esterblud who led the escape.

Phillo glared down at the people below him, his fury barely contained. The two Borrs who guarded the barracks overnight were on their knees, tied to the rails of the platform. Instead of publicly accepting the surrender of Queen Darrca, the Borr leader would now go after her. He intended to extract a vengeful revenge on the few remaining Rarfell guards. When Phillo looked over at the audience, he recognized some of the Gallaeci families who entered Cymeer with his victory. They stood in a small group separated from the villagers.

"To my Gallaeci friends who've lost their homes, you will take the buildings of those Rarfell people who resisted our takeover." He looked over at the line of village elders.

"To ensure your path to Facarm, you must swear an oath of alliance to me. Now knell before me!"

Slowly, the crowd went to their knees. Those who were too slow found themselves pushed down by nearby Borr guards, who joined them in kneeling. However, one elder in the middle of the crowd remained standing. His frail body puffed up as his weathered face scowled at Phillo.

"I'm Orak. Rarfell blood runs through my veins and I'll not submit to you and your Gallaeci scum." He turned to the crowd of onlookers, who stared up at him. Borrs hurried toward him, hindered by the kneeling people in their way.

"Those of Cymeer, rise with me and show this…"

The first guard to reach the elder started beating him as more Borrs arrived.

"No, don't kill him," Phillo bellowed out after glancing at his advisors, who stood behind him.

"Bring this man closer."

The guards forced the elder forward while the crowd grew restless. They stood. Sarcam, who stood next to Yartha, moved forward to direct his men. He pulled his sword. Yartha gave Sarcam his war mallet as he went to the other side of the platform. A blood covered linen cloth enclosed Yartha's head. Phillo slammed his weapon on the railing to get the crowd's attention.

"It's clear you peasants need a lesson. The winds of fate come your way. Take that man to the pen of the horuks."

Pushing Orak along, the Borrs cleared a path to the barracks field where a fenced arena now stood. Phillo caught the attention of the audience again with his mallet.

"To show you that my rule is fair, look at these men in front of me. These are the Borr men who failed in their duties," Phillo explained. "Now, they will receive their sentence."

As one prisoner yelled out his allegiance to Facarm, the new overlord swung his heavy mallet. The sound of his voice stopped with a sickening crack, followed by blood and gore scattering across the crowd. The next execution proceeded just as swiftly. The silence from the crowd surprised Phillo. He scanned their dirty faces.

"I've punished those who failed in their orders. Now, look at those who cannot accept the rule of Phillo." He pointed to the pen where the guards pushed Orak past the gate and closed it. After opening the door to the attached building, the men climbed to safety over the rails as the large flightless birds emerged.

Intrigued and fearful, the audience slowly gathered around the pen as the creatures squawked. Cocking their gigantic heads, the birds immediately spotted Orak. One horuk opened its sharp hooked beak and screeched impatiently. Standing taller than their prey, the birds crouched and began circling the man, who stood stoically in the center of the pen.

The man visibly shook as he observed the creatures which circled as they sized up their prey. When the man pulled his dagger, the guards laughed. They began taunting him. One bird rushed the man from behind, catching Orak in his leg. The attack brought blood, which excited both creatures. They moved faster around the victim, rushing in to nip at their prey. The horuk behind the elder jumped up and extended its sharp talons. Orak dropped with a loud groan and his robe shredded. His dagger swing at the bird came far too late as the creature trotted away. However, the other horuk came in and caught Orak by the side. Instantly, the powerful bird lifted the screaming man from the ground. Then it flung its victim to the ground. Instantly, horuks cut into the man's belly. Screaming, Orak thrashed around while the birds gutted him alive. Cries and yells come from the crowd as they witnessed the cruel death. Gradually, silence fell across the crowd as the savage birds continued feeding after Orak finally died.

"Those who oppose the rule of Phillo must suffer my wrath. We wipe the past and bring forth the strongest to lead the kingdom." The new overlord of Rarfell told the audience. He turned to his advisors on the platform.

"Now I travel to take my revenge on those who took Darrca. Before I'm through, everyone will know there is no safe place for here in Rarfell. Everyone who assisted in her escape I'll roast on an open fire."

Phillo stomped away, leaving Yartha to hurry after him. He followed the Borr leader down the steps. The two men went toward a line of Borrs lined up on either side of Phillo's armored ossane.

"I wish to join you," Yartha told Phillo.

Phillo glanced back at him while continuing his rapid pace. "Do you have vengeance on your mind?"

"Of course, that Esterblud came back from the grave and took what was mine! I'll place his head on a pike for all of Cymeer to see," Yartha vowed. "If you agree, Sarcam will maintain order here."

Phillo grimly smiled at the comment, ordering the Borr guard next to him to dismount.

"That is good! For if you do not kill this Esterblud, I'll place your head on the pike in his place." The Borr leader swung up on his saddle. He looked down at the surprised Yartha.

"Don't look shocked that I live by the words of Facarm. You left a wounded man to seek his retribution against you. I taught you better than that. Since you made an error in judgment, then you must correct it by confronting your enemy directly."

He turned his mount and started for the gate. Yartha got on the saddle of his ossane. His fury at Urith and Mekan remained, but he suddenly recalled his conversation with Phillo at daybreak. He found the body of the dead guard who died by the queen's hand. The woman slipped out of Phillo's bedroom while he slept. As he dug his heels into the ossane's flanks, Yartha grew bitter.

The great Phillo doesn't make an error! Only those who follow him.

The sun rose over the small farm of Tobal as he pulled the blue eggs from under his caged *eartals*. Occasionally, he felt the sharp prick from a black beak. After so many seasons of dealing with the wild brown birds with their long purple tail feathers, the farmer barely reacted. He moved the upset creature to the side and took the eggs. Letting himself out of the pen, Tobal noticed two ossanes coming along the back trail to his farm.

Instantly curious, he held his hand against the glare of the sun as the animals drew closer. He recognized the blue tunics and grew nervous. Even on his remote farm, news of the Borr takeover reached him. Nearly dropping the eggs held in the folds of his brown robe, the small, pudgy man looked around for his scythe. Seeing the farm tool propped against this house, Tobal walked over while monitoring the riders.

When he recognized Hera, Tobal relaxed and waved to him. He didn't know the other riders. Then, the farmer noticed each ossane carried two people, including a blonde woman riding behind Hera. When the riders came to a stop, their mounts were close to exhaustion. Hera nearly collapsed when he finally got off his ossane. Tobal rushed over, then pointed the group to his water trough, where the riders and ossanes drank.

The farmer waited for the bad news as he kept glancing at the woman's blood-stained tunic that scarcely covered her naked body. Something about her looked familiar.

"Come inside, I'll get food for you," Tobal waved him inside. "Hera, you need rest. You look terrible."

"You're not the first to notice," the guard joked, then noticed his old friend eyeing his companions. Hera introduced them and then he told Tobal the news.

"You probably don't know yet, but the towns of our land have fallen to the Borrs, who have the other Gallaeci tribes coming in now to join them. Their leader will come after Darrca. I'm not sure if they'll come this way, but we can only stay for water and food if you have enough."

"My queen, I heard there was trouble with the Gallaeci from a friend who farms nearby," Tobal turned to her.

"I'm so sorry for your difficulty. You can have anything you need." Tobal eagerly went to the small wooden hamlet, dropping an egg on the way. Darrca smiled at the farmer's excitement to help as she followed him inside.

Esart worked on feeding the ossanes while Darrca, Parca, and Hera sat around the hearth in the center of the building. Tobal pulled a piece of smoked meat from the wall, handing it to Parca. The farmer took a pitcher of *holiar* from his counter and sat the fermented honey drink it by the fire to warm while they ate. The remaining Rarfell leaders ate with haste while briefly retelling their escape with the help of Urith. The queen remained quiet, letting Parca do most of the talking.

Tobal went to a chest near his bed of slats and straw. He pulled on a coarse brown robe, along with breeches and stockings. After he sat the clothes on the floor next to Darrca, the farmer went to his counter.

"Those clothes will let you blend into the other country people," he told the queen while he worked on filling a leather bag with more of his dried food. "I'm afraid I have only one ossane, but you may take it."

Darrca observed the man, trying to determine his age. His weathered chubby face and gray hair made him look older. His stout arms showed the heavy manual work he endured.

"No, keep it. We can't speed up our progress with just one. Where do these garments come from?" She ran her hand over the coarse wool fabric, which carried the fresh scent of wood from the trunk.

"They were my wife's." Tobal replied quickly. "I have no need of them."

Without a word, Queen Darrca went outside by the water trough and stripped off the tunic she wore. She splashed the cold water across her upper body, cleaning off the remnants of blood while Esart left her to her work. He cast a longing glance before entering the hamlet.

As Darrca finished changing clothes, the rest of her group came outside carrying the supplies. Esart was busily stuffing his mouth with meat.

"We've got a hard ride ahead of us," Hera told Darrca. "But we should arrive before the sun drops from the sky."

She looked at the exhausted guard, wondering how much longer he could go.

"You're barely able to stand. Do you think you can ride the reminder of the day?"

He gave her a half-hearted grin. "There's no option."

"He'll ride with me and I'll take care of him. Where are we going?" Parca asked after getting on an ossane.

He held out a hand to Hera. The leader struggled to get on the mount, but finally pulled in behind him.

"I've got a place where we can rest before we take the path to Cahmais. No one will think to look for us at my old home. No trail goes there, and few remember it exists," Hera explained while he watched Esart and Darrca got on their ossane.

"Too bad we can't have a rain help cover our tracks," Esart looked at the bright sky.

Tobal handed the bags with supplies to Esart. The queen placed her hand on the farmer's shoulder.

"I hope to repay your generosity in the future."

Tobal blushed and thanked her.

"After you leave Hera's old homestead, take the mountain pass of Savaor to Cahmais. No Gallaeci travel through there since few people use that path."

He waved as the Rarfell group galloped away.

~~~

The morning light guided Urith and his comrades to the road after a long night moving to woods. While Mekan showed them a shortcut that allowed them to avoid the main road, progress was slow because of the dark path. To make things worse, the ossane could only handle two riders. It left Dutra jogging along while they followed the winding route. As he hurried to keep up with the ossane, the boy showed Urith an unexpected grit during the night. The Esterblud remained hesitant about coming close to the main roads, knowing the Borrs would sweep the area. They couldn't risk being seen.

"We can't go to your home. That'll be the first place they look," the warrior reminded Mekan as she guided them out of the forest.

"Of course, I'm not a fool. I'm taking us to my uncle," she explained. "We have to take this road for a short way before we take a back trail to Tobal's farm."

"That'll be the second place they look. We already know some of your people sided with the Borrs." He slowed the ossane to let Dutra catch his breath. It also allowed him to better manage the intense pain caused by Yartha's mallet on his chest.
~~~

"We're only getting supplies. Tobal will give us an ossane as well. We can't have Dutra running with us the whole way."

While Urith believed she was joking, her exasperated tone made it difficult to tell.

"It makes as much sense as anything else I've heard." He looked down at the boy.

"What say you? Can you hold out?"

Dutra nodded; his weary expression brightened momentarily.

"I'll make it."

The Esterblud spurred the ossane on.

"Again, I have to thank you for saving my hide," Urith told Mekan.

She remained quiet at his comment. He didn't bother asking her about her presence with Yartha. Urith witnessed the longing looks coming from the Gallaeci in the past.

"Do you still want to see Eran?" the warrior finally asked.

"Only after I see Yartha dead!" Her voice trembled with pain and fury. "There's the trail to Tobal's farm."

"That's what I expected!" Urith nodded with approval as he followed her directions.

The trio reached Tobal's farm as the farmer came out of his ossane stable. His eyes widened at the sight of the big man wearing a too-small robe. Each step of the mount caused a black helmet to clank against a shield while a boy ran beside the ossane. When Urith came alongside Tobal, he immediately recognized Mekan.

"What's happened?"

"We need your help. There are Gallaeci after us. Can we get supplies and another ossane?" Mekan asked while sliding off their mount.

"Sure…tell me what's happened?"

"We don't have much time. You've not heard about my father?" Mekan followed Topal to his house.

Urith listened to the conversation as he gingerly got off the ossane. The woman quickly told Topal about her ordeal, including the death of the farmer's brother. To his credit, the man took the news stoically. He led the ossane to the water trough, then pulled off a leather bladder from the saddle to fill with the liquid. Dutra came next to Urith and dunked his head in the water before taking several long drinks.

"You did well," the warrior praised the boy. He slipped out the crude dagger retrieved from one of the dead Borrs that was stuck in his belt.

"Here, take this! Once I get my dagger back from Yartha, I'll show you a proper Sgian weapon."

As droplets of water came off the boy's brown hair, his beaming smile showed crooked teeth. His devious expression caused Urith to sneer.

"Alright, what is going on?"

Dutra's hand went to his side and, with a quick flash, he held out Urith's dagger.

"During your fight, I took this off Yartha."

The Esterblud laughed, surprised at missing the weapon on the boy as he traded daggers with Dutra.

"I need to keep a closer eye on you!"

He glanced over to see Mekan watching them. Then, she went inside the house with her uncle. Urith ordered Dutra to feed the ossane, then he struggled to pull off the smelly robe he wore.

"…left earlier this morning," Tobal stopped when the Esterblud entered the room.

"This is Urith," Mekan told him. "He's helped me to escape, along with Hera and the others. We're following them."

"What's an Esterblud helping Rarfell guards?" Suspicion filled his question.

"Because I was bored!" Urith gave his sneer grin. "And Mekan wants to see the world."

The woman glared at him for the joke.

"Can we get some food until we reach a safe place?" Mekan asked Tobal. He pointed her to the bench by the hearth.

"Of course, but are you following Hera? You know…"

"We need enough to get to Esterblud," Urith interrupted. "Once there, I can go to King Penhda about supporting those left to fit the Gallaeci."

"That makes sense," Tobal agreed quickly. He went to the wall where dried *duelill* meat hung. "You can keep off the main road and go through the mountain pass into your lands."

"I'm following Hera," Mekan declared.

"For what reason? There's only three Rarfell guards free. They'll be going to Cahmais." Urith grumbled.

"You didn't hear what Tobal told me. Queen Darcca's with Hera and his men." She took the meat that her uncle brought to them.

"And why do you want to join them? You have no skills with the blade or spear." The warrior looked for her response. Her quick glare suggested he knew the answer.

"That's true, but I'm a Cyer and my loyalty remains to the clan. The queen and Hera will gather forces to destroy Phillo. I want to be there when they do." Her narrowed eyes betrayed vengeance. "You know I want Yartha's heart removed from his living body."

Urith nodded.

"Probably more than I do. Then it appears we're going to catch up with Darrca."

He didn't see the frown cross Tobal's face at the news.

"Mekan, you shouldn't involve yourself in this. Go to Esterblud and avoid the danger. Once the queen takes back the land, I'll come for you."

The woman looked up. "Uncle, that's very good of you, but I've decided about this."

"But I know my brother wanted your safety. We spoke about this before. You can't disregard his wishes, or mine." Tobal insisted. "I'm afraid you're not thinking about the needs of your family."

Mekan stood and handed the dried meat.

"My uncle and I must speak in private," she told him. "Tobal's already agreed we can have one of his ossanes. You and Dutra can get it ready for our journey."

Urith took the food and left them. He found Dutra coming to the building. Handing the boy their rations, he told him to put it on his ossane.

"Come out to the pen. We'll saddle another one so you don't slow us down anymore." He gave him his sneer grin.

When Mekan finally left the house, she carried two leather bags. Urith caught her determined expression as she joined them.

"I take it you're traveling to find Hera?" He took the bags and tied them to the saddle as Dutra left to get the other ossane.

"Yes, my uncle fully understands my feelings now. I told him to take my father's ossanes as payment for the one we're taking. Do you still want to go to Esterblud?"

Urith looked over the top of the saddle at her. Torn by his thoughts of helping the queen and his responsibility to get the word back to Penhda, the warrior decided on the only solution available.

"I believe it's the best option. With the queen going to Cahmais, the action invites interference from the Aberffraw, which King Penhda will not accept. I will join you to speak with Darcca about this problem."

She stroked the animal's long neck.

"I've heard about the wars between your kingdoms. We're not part of such things."

The Esterblud handed her the reins as Dutra arrived with the other mount.

"Well, your people are now involved. Once Penhda hears about the Gallaeci and their overthrow of Rarfell, he will send many warriors. It will not turn out well for anyone."

Mekan waited as Urith took the reins from Dutra and lifted himself on the mount. She noticed how he grimaced in pain from his movement.

"Are you badly injured?"

He nodded to the other ossane, ignoring her question.

"Let's go find your queen. It shouldn't be hard to follow two overloaded ossanes."

As they rode away, Tobal came out of his house. His bitter expression remained as he watched Mekan until she was no longer in sight.

~~~

Darrca arrived with her escort at a small shack as the night crept over the sky. Pulling off a rutted trail overgrown with vegetation, she followed the ossane of Parca. On the way to the abandoned shack, Hera told her that his parents once had a farm, which they abandoned during Gallaeci raids when
~~~

he was young. A joint band of warriors under the control of Darrca's uncle drove the Gallaeci from the land, but Hera never returned.

They pulled their ossanes under the heavy tangle of overgrown fruit trees that were blooming. The sweet smell reminded Hera of his youth, and he smiled for a moment.

"This is a perfect place to rest," he spoke as the queen came next to him. "Riders can't get at us easily. Our enemy will have to come for us on foot. The woods now cover the fields my father used to farm."

Darrca looked over the area and nodded. She decided not to point out that an overwhelming number of warriors on foot would still destroy them. She ordered Hera to rest. With little resistance to the idea, Hera accepted Parca's went inside the dilapidated building.

Esart told the queen to find shelter inside. Parca exited the building while chewing on a piece of jerky.

"I made a fire inside. Take the bedroll from the saddle. My brother and I will guard the area, just in case the Borrs stumble upon us."

Weariness filled the woman as she nodded.

Darrca carried the blanket rolled with something inside to the ruins. She passed by Hera, whose eyes were closed. Finding a place near the growing fire coming from the old hearth, the woman unrolled the bedroll. Three swords and two daggers fell out, their clanging sound caused Hera to open his eyes.

"That Esterblud must have killed Borr fighters for their ossanes. I've heard the warriors of his tribe keep weapons for their value and status when he returns to Esterblud." The man explained as he watched her run her finger along the pommel.

"They're crudely made compared to those forged by our blacksmith," the woman observed, then she glanced over.

"What about your decision to leave one ossane in that forest back at Cymeer? Do you believe Urith will survive?"

"It was not a smart decision, given the odds. The Esterblud will never make it out of Cymeer, but I owed Urith for my life."

She moved the swords from the blanket and laid them beside her.

"Go to sleep. We'll talk in the morning." Daccra stared at the weapons with a puzzled expression before taking the blanket.

As the woman rolled out the blanket, she remembered the last time she saw the Esterblud. The sight of Urith hanging on to the ossane as he fell from the cliff replayed in her mind. Shaking her head, the woman lay on the ground, believing sleep would soon come. However, as she lay on the hard-packed ground, the queen's thoughts came back to the warrior. The woman couldn't believe he survived such a fall. Aside from his disfiguring scar, the young man carried the same swagger all warriors had. But something in his gray eyes carried a sadness along with wisdom beyond his age. She knew the reason behind the look. Daccra saw it before in the distant look given by men hardened by ferocious battles.

When the skalds traveled through Rarfell, the queen enjoyed listening to their stories when they gathered by the king's hearth. The Clovel Destroyer's name came out several times in the retelling of his battles against monsters. One story even claimed the man tried to enter the underworld to save the spirit of his warrior father and his dead wife. The sheer audacity of that story made her discount it. But now, she could believe it happened.

Darrca used the skalds to surround herself with the wisdom and strength of such men because she never experienced hardships. However, once she returned to power, the queen would encourage her people to learn from people like the Esterbluds. Her recent experiences left her with a strange need for revenge, along with a thirst for knowledge about running a kingdom.

Given Urith's escape from certain death, she wondered if the Fates protected the Esterblud. If not, it still made for another thrilling story about the warrior. She smiled to herself as she pictured the skalds singing around the hearth about a queen retaking her lands back from Phillo.

They'll talk about my bloody vengeance upon him!

The sound of ossane hoofs broke the woman from her thoughts. A chill enveloped her body.

Borrs!

Darrca and Hera heard Parca yell out for the riders to stop.

"Quit shouting, you fool!" Urith's growling voice entered the shack. "You can see that fire in the house from this path. You'd already be dead if I wanted to kill you."

Despite her weariness, Darrca unconsciously smiled and lifted herself from the ground. When she stepped out of the building, the last rays of sunlight showed Urith still on an ossane. He continued to berate the brothers about leaving a fire going while the Borrs tracked them. On the other ossane was a pretty woman sliding off the saddle while a small boy held the reins.

"Do you always order strangers around?" Darrca stepped to the side of the warrior's ossane. Her good-humored expression caught Mekan's eye.

"Fair queen, it's good to see you made it." His eyes lit up at her sight. "You have more volunteers."

She smiled at him. "It appears the Fates regard you as worthy." She looked at Mekan and Dutra and her expression turned somber.

"I appreciate a jest, but we need experienced fighters."

Urith swung his leg over the saddle and Darrca noticed his stiff movement, along with an attempt to hide the grimace on his face.

Hera joined the queen.

"It's about time you showed up. Do you have many following you?" He asked Urith.

The Esterblud shook his head. "I can't be sure of anything. My guide took us on a long route."

He gave his sneer grin as Mekan stepped next to Hera. The woman's face brightened at Hera's presence, then she frowned.

"Are you alright?"

"The Borrs did the best they could, but I'm tougher than they expected." His lopsided smile faded as he looked down at his injured hands. She noticed his thumbs and Mekan place her hand on his shoulder.

Darrca watched the exchange, and she noticed Urith's sidelong glance at the sympathetic attraction between the two.

"I hope you have a plan to get back to Cymeer." Urith turned to Darrca. "That's the reason that I'm here. I know we need rest, but I suggest we take some time to discuss this now."

The queen nodded, then she went toward the ruins.

"Hera, let's put something around that fire in case the Esterblud is correct about the Borrs searching for us at night."

The night turned chilly as Parca remained on guard near the trail, lightly dozing while he leaned against a tree. He glanced enviously at the dark hut where the rest of his group huddled around the embers of the fire.

"I understand your concerns, Urith. We have no guarantee that the king of Cahmais will help us. However, the mountain pass is the quickest way out of Rarfell," Hera looked over at the queen.

"I can't believe King Penhda would invade my kingdom," Darrca interjected. "The Gallaeci are a larger threat than Aberffraw warriors coming here. Besides, I'll decide the allies I want to join me when I return!"

Urith listened, his expression skeptical.

"Queen Darrca, I'm telling you how my overlord will react when he finds his worst enemy drawing close to Esterblud lands. Before, you didn't accept my advice about going to Esterblud. Instead, you went to Eleb," he reminded her.

Darrca's eyes expressed her instant fury.

"It's not my fault that I trusted the words of the same man who betrayed both of us. You act like our people know nothing of our land or our allies. You're not the king! I won't take insults from an Esterblud."

Urith's eyes narrowed as his temper rose.

"Darrca, I'm not a diplomat and I won't say things to make you feel better. I expect you to want the truth. You have three warriors to oppose the Borrs and Hera remains injured. You go to Cahmais and King Penhda will intervene in your land. The Esterblud are not friends with the Gallaeci either, so you risk your people's misery if a war breaks out between Cahmais and Esterblud over your land. You might not have a kingdom after that."

The man and the woman stared at each other for a moment. Hera finally interceded.

"Queen Darrca, what Urith says carries truth," he glanced at the warrior. "While we might find a few more fighters on a route to Esterblud, such a journey will add another week to get there. That means a greater risk and assumes that the Borrs don't find us. Plus, we know Gallaeci families come from the mountain pass to Esterblud. We might run into them."

He paused and looked at Urith.

"Is that not correct?"

Grudgingly, Urith nodded. He picked up a bladder to take a drink.

"What you say is true. But I believe it's still easier to gather those willing to fight for Rarfell on the way. Sitting in Cahmais with a few people does not make an army to return. Ask yourself who will leave Rarfell to join you once the Gallaeci hear you are in Cahmais?"

He turned to the queen.

"Hera and I agree that there's a risk in my idea. Perhaps it's too dangerous. However, you must know all the options to weigh in your decisions. Penhda once told my father that to give advice means the advisor must keep his tongue as sharp as his sword. It does a ruler no good for a counselor to agree when their heart doesn't believe it."

"Then the decision is not obvious. Your idea carries significant risk to us. We lose all should the Borrs take us," Darrca stated firmly.

She expected the Esterblud to argue further. He surprised her by leaning against the trunk of the tree, his eyes never leaving hers. His expression appeared relaxed, almost bemused. Then she understood.

He recognized there's no best choice, but he wants me to know my options. He wants to stay in Rarfell to fight the Borrs!

As the tension slowly abated, the queen reconsidered the problems of bringing either Cahmais or Esterblud into the conflict. Then she glimpsed Dutra yawn while he rolled his blanket into his pillow.

"Look, we're tired, which makes the correct decision difficult. I'm torn by the advice. My instinct is to stay here and fight. However, I must have the Cyer and the Rarfell elder's support. Phillo told me he's already spread rumors in the kingdom about me and my brother. With Lerah under Gallaeci control, the better strategy seems to leave the land and return with an army."

The queen slumped wearily.

"Perhaps we should get sleep," Mekan spoke up for the first time. "A decision isn't necessary tonight, is it?"

Glances shared among the group confirmed her thoughts. Silence filled the room before Darrca agreed with Mekan. Hera smiled at the farmer's daughter. He noticed Urith observing him.

~~~

Phillo and Yartha arrived at the crossroads close to Mekan's farm as the sun was setting. The leader of the Borrs showed his impatience at their slow progress as they waited for the scouts to return. In a nearby line, his men waited impatiently as well. Many of the Borrs wore brown hooded robes with their bows slung over their shoulders and short swords hanging from their belts. Only the few leaders and the scouts had either chain mail or leather armor on, and they carried swords or mallets. They also carried shields on their back.
~~~

"The Esterblud will go back to his land. You should take men and follow the main road that way. There's only one ossane, and we know they cannot outrun you to the border."

"I want to wait on that man who is from Cymeer. He thinks the woman will lead Urith to her farm." Yartha commented. "It's possible they are following the escaped Rarfell men."

Phillo grunted before downing more heathmead from a bladder.

"I don't like it. We're not making fast progress by waiting. I want to enjoy my vengeance on that bitch." He turned to one of his men. "Have those men tracking our prey make torches so we can follow at night."

"We risk losing their trail along the streams," the Borr scout advised.

Phillo glared at him.

"I'll not wait another day to kill those who escaped. Now do as I order."

It was long after dark when Tobal heard ossanes outside his home. He stepped outside to see men holding torches as they followed the trail. The Borrs swarmed around his house when they noticed Tobal at the front door.

"Who came through earlier today?" One rider shouted.

Tobal stepped out to get a look at the men. The tattooed faces of many fighters coldly looked down at the farmer. He hid his shaking hands inside the caped robe he wore.

"It was a boy with a big man and a local woman heading to Cahmais."

"I don't care about them. I want the Rarfell Guards on those two ossanes were following." A growling voice came from an enormous shadow that galloped forward. Phillo rode into the light of the torches.

Tobal's eyes widened at the sight. He'd heard the rumors of terrible deaths brought by the man astride the black ossane.

"They went on that path," the farmer finally stammered out.

The scout nodded agreement when Phillo glanced at him.

"The blonde woman with them. Do you know her?" Yartha asked.

Tobal shook his head.

"When did they pass through?" Phillo leaned over the saddle horn to pull off a leather bladder.

"They…they left before midday. They were in a hurry."

Phillo laughed, then took a drink.

"We'll stay for the night. Get us food and drink, farmer!"

As the Borrs dismounted and pulled their ossanes to the water, Tobal hurried inside. He quickly pulled the paltry amount of hanging meat from the wall. Phillo entered the hovel with Yartha, along with other Gallaeci fighters. They gathered around the embers of the fire, ordering Tobal to bring them the food.

"I'm afraid that I don't have much for so many," the farmer told them. "It will take a while for a stew. How about drink instead?"

Phillo nodded and Tobal went to the cask holding his holiar and poured the contents into a pitcher. Yartha took the pitcher from him.

"Give us those mugs. When we leave, you'll get a reward for your trouble."

Tobal thanked him before hurrying to get all the clay and wooden cups he had. Then, the farmer went to sit on his bed in the corner. He listened to the conversation.

"The ones we seek will not make good time with overloaded mounts. We'll get some sleep, then head out before the sun rises," Phillo told those near him. He finished the mug and licked his lips.

"Not bad, farmer. Do you have any more?"

Tobal nodded, telling him about an unfinished cask in the barn.

"Well, get it ready for us when we wake! The Borrs expect service from those who serve us." Phillo growled at him. "Now, tell me about what the queen and her friends talked about while they were here."

Tobal scanned the deadly stares coming from the men. His hands started shaking again. Then he told them everything. When he finished, Phillo nodded absently.

"They intend to enlist King Asgurd against us. The bitch has more brains than I expected. I'll have to ensure she pays dearly for such dangerous thinking."

Tobal remained quiet. He'd heard about Gallaeci bandits being executed on sight by the Aberffraw warriors.

"The king of Cahmais might consider an invasion of Rarfell should Darrca go to him," Phillo stated to Yartha. "What paths run to Cahmais from here?"

"They'll go through the mountain pass of Savaor," Tobal interrupted.

Then he smiled.

"That was the way I suggested. I also sent the Esterblud who came through to follow that direction. He intends to get the queen to change her mind and go to Esterblud."

Phillo smiled and glanced at Yartha.

"Why would you send the Esterblud after the queen?" Yartha stepped next to the farmer.

"Like you, Urith thinks the Cahmais king will send his warriors here," Tobal replied. "He's confused Mekan. She betrayed her father. My brother promised her to me."

"I see. You want the Esterblud's woman." Phillo smirked at the idea. He stood and went to the one bed in the room. As he sat down on the straw mattress, he looked at the farmer.

"I'll sleep here. You will wake me before the sun rises." He leaned back on the small bed that creaked under his weight.

"You'll see that cooperating with the Gallaeci can bring you great fortune."

"I seek nothing in return but Mekan." Tobal told him.

Phillo smiled.

"I believe in making woman happy in their marriages."

As the sun peeked over the western horizon, the Borrs waited in two lines of ossanes near the home of Tobal. They had already stripped the farm of all the grain for their mounts from the farm.

Inside the hovel, Yartha ordered Tobal to fill his bags with the drink. The farmer worked quickly while giving Yartha a fake smile. He talked as he poured the last of the holiar into the bags. While he poured the liquid, he didn't see Yartha's irritated expression.

"When you kill the Esterblud, please return Mekan to me." Tobal implored the Gallaeci. The big man smiled back and took the bags, hoisting them on his shoulder.

"Come on Yartha, I grew impatient," Phillo's voice came into the room from outside.

"I see you smoke *ulcath*. Fill me a pipe for me and bring a burning stick," Yartha ordered Tobal as he walked out to his mount.

"I bring drink and entertainment," he hands the bag to Phillo, who glared at him before he tied the bag to his saddle

"I don't have time for this." The Borr leader growled.

"But I'm following your orders," Yartha replied with a grin. He drank the heathmead thirstily, then tied the bag to his saddle.

"You told this farmer that a great fortune awaits. As a follower of Facarm, we Borrs give sacrifices to Caruun."

Tobal returned with a pipe and the burning piece of wood. After lighting the pipe, Yartha pitched the burning wood on the thatched roof of the man's home.

"What are you doing?" The frantic farmer tried to knock the burning piece away, but the larger man grabbed him by the shoulder. With precision and speed, the Gallaeci swung around his mallet. The weapon struck the man in the leg, sending him to the ground.

"Phillo promised you great fortune," Yartha stated as he slammed the man's leg with his weapon. Tobal screamed out in agony while those watching the attack heard the gut-wrenching crack of the broken leg over the spreading fire.

"Our overlord also ordered death for all those who helped the queen escape." Yartha ordered a nearby Borr guard over. After they picked up the injured man, the two men threw him through the door of the burning building.

"Your fortune is to join the other unworthy wretches in Caruun's realm!"

The screaming Tobal tried to crawl to the door as Yartha slammed the door shut. He pushed the wooden bench in front of the door before the growing intense heat from the fire forced Yartha to back away. He went to his ossane and pulled himself on the saddle.

"Just following your orders, my lord." The Gallaeci smirked.

Phillo shook his head. "Your strange sense of humor always makes me laugh!"

The overlord turned his mount and led the Borrs away from the farm. As the line of riders galloped away, the frantic screams from the farmer continued until the fully engulfed thatch roof collapsed on the injured Tobal.

Chapter 6: Pass of Savaor

As the rest of the Rarfell survivors slept, Parca stood guard near the hovel. He stomped on the ground in the vain hope of shaking off the drowsiness. The dawn sky remained behind the mountain range still, leaving the area in a hazy purple hue. He heard a noise from the ruins and turned to see Dutra coming toward him. A smile came to the Rarfell's face. He remembered the foul expression on the lad when Urith gave him the chore of saddling the ossanes in the morning.

The young man passed by without a word, heading into the tangle of vegetation near the remains of a barn. Parca continued along a path around the house. The guard longed for the warmth of his blanket, even on a hard-packed floor. He grumbled under his breath.

"Why am I doing this? Cursed Borrs aren't riding at night."

Suddenly, he heard running footsteps behind him. When Parca turned, he found Dutra nearly on him.

"There's men out there!" He gasped out. "I heard ossanes moving."

"Are you sure?" Parca placed his finger to his lips as Dutra nodded. They heard the whiny of an ossane in the distance.

"Alright, keep quiet and go wake the others. Tell them to move fast and get out to the ossanes. I'll have them ready." He grabbed Dutra as he tried to run away. "Don't forget to grab all the food we can."

With his instructions, the boy sped away with Parca on his heels. Dutra ran into the ruins while the guard continued to the ossanes. He found them tied to a tree and threw a saddle on the closest mount. As he worked, the sound of men on their mounts reached him. The noise remained distant and moving parallel with his position.

Inside the shack, Urith woke at the sound of Dutra's footsteps. Still wearing his chain mail, he had his Clovel Sword out when the boy entered the room. In the dim light of embers glowing in the hearth, the warrior instantly recognized trouble in Dutra's expression. He scrambled from his blanket, ignoring his chest pain from the movement. At nearly the same instant, Hera rolled out of his blanket.

"Parca's getting the ossanes ready. He says to hurry and bring the bags." The young man's excitement was palpable.

"Get your blanket and grab the water bags." Urith glanced at Hera, who woke Mekan.

"I'll help Parca outside," the Esterblud grabbed his gear.

Esart and Darrca overheard Dutra's excitement and were already gathering their items. Urith quickly pulled on his helmet and flipped his shield over his back, hooking it to his baudrik belt. As he met up with the queen, Darrca smiled.

"You left your captured swords." She held the blanket wrapped with them in her arms.

Urith's sneer grin spread across his face. "I suspect we'll need them. But these are for you. I remember that you're pretty handy with these."

He placed two daggers he captured from the Borrs on top of the blanket.

Urith missed her surprised expression as he hurried away. She watched him duck to leave through the doorway. The man appeared happy at the thought of fighting. She heard of the Esterblud's fervent wish to die in battle. While all warriors desired the afterlife inside Haligulf, it was the first time she witnessed such a personal zeal for the idea. Darrca felt a hand on her shoulder.

"We must hurry," Hera reminded her.

Parca nearly finished with the last ossane's saddle as Urith arrived. The Rarfell Guard waved the Esterblud closer.

"I hear them moving to cut us off from the path to Cahmais," Parca whispered. "We need another way out of here. I suspect the main body is coming fast."

"I'll take these ossanes and get them loaded. Hera should know where we're going."

Urith quietly led the ossanes to the clearing by the trail where Hera and Esart were trying to get on their leather armor. Darrca and Mekan came out carrying saddle bags while Dutra hurried after them. The group started packing the ossanes when they heard the crashing of a mount speeding through the underbrush.

Almost instantly, war cries sounded from the area where Parca came rushing up on his mount. He was about to say something when a volley of arrows rained down on the group. One arrow struck Parca in the shoulder, coming down through his collarbone. He nearly fell from his mount as he clung to the saddle with his legs.

Ignoring the next round of raining projectiles, Urith threw Dutra behind Mekan, who just climbed on an ossane.

"Get us of here!" He yelled to Hera.

The Rarfell leader slide behind Darrca while Urith pulled himself behind the wounded Parca. Hera led the group into the tangle of fruit trees, forcing them to go into a single file and passing close to the ruins of Hera's old home. The last volley of arrows mostly struck the ruins. However, one projectile landed into the ossane that Esart guided. The ossane shrieked, but the guard kept control as they followed Hera into the nearly dark shadows of the forest.

The increasing daylight allowed Hera to see a path away from his homestead. As they went deeper into the woods, the landmarks were far different from what he remembered. The group headed toward the mountains they saw occasionally between trees. From the destruction in the underbrush along the narrow trail, Hera recognized he led them along a *rangifer* path. The two horned hogs rooted among the low hung bushes, eating their favorite tubular roots. Normally, the animal trails led to human paths.

Bringing up the rear of the column, Urith took over the reins from Parca, who leaned over, placing one hand on the long-necked animal to support him. He groaned as Urith took hold of the arrow, still stuck in the guard.

"Grit your teeth, I'm breaking the shaft," the Esterblud warned as they galloped along.

Almost immediately, he snapped the wood. The man in front of him quivered, then wobbled in the saddle. Urith grabbed him with one hand, keeping the man from falling off.

"Breathe through the pain," Urith quietly encouraged him as he looked over the shaft. "Pull it out through your chest. We'll get moss on it when we get to water."

Parca nodded, then faltered in the saddle again when he placed his hand around the iron arrow tip.

"Curse you, toughen up!" The Esterblud behind him growled.

Mekan overheard parts of the conversation and glanced back. She noticed the words had an effect as Parca's expression turned defiant. Despite the ducking and weaving as they rode along, Parca forced himself to pull the rest of the arrow from his chest. His pathetic grunt reached Urith, who steadied Parca on the saddle as he sucked in deep breaths of air.

"You're a *bwar*!" Parca told Urith.

"I've been called worse than an ossane's rump," he replied. "Take the reins and keep up with the others."

The Rarfell Guard nodded as yells broke out on their left. A wave of several Borrs on their mounts crashed through the foliage after the column. Hera spurred his mount and took a barely visible path away from the onslaught while shouting for the others to follow. Mekan and Esart came in behind the leader of their column. However, Gallaeci riders caught up with the struggling mount holding Parca and Urith. The dense vegetation on either side of the path kept the rest of Gallaeci from rushing ahead and getting in front of the small group. Instead, they pulled in behind Urith and Parca. The Esterblud fended off those who drew close using his sword. However, Urith couldn't get a good swing with Parca sitting in front of him.

The overloaded ossanes meant the escaping people couldn't outrun their pursuers. Avoiding a low-hanging branch which slowed the group of Rarfell, a Borr drew close enough to swing his mallet. The weapon struck Urith's shield, hanging on his back. Urith swung around with his sword, his blade struck into the body of the ossane and the leg of his enemy. Blood spurted out from the wounds as the injured animal halted abruptly. The action pitched the rider from his saddle.

Parca turned the mount, barely avoiding a tree. His action broke up the group of pursuers. When he glanced back, only two of the Borrs remained close.

"We can't outrun these mounts," the Rarfell man said. "And I can't keep up with Esart."

"Then, we'll cut them off and I'll take them," Urith spoke into Pacra's ear. "Turn hard to the left when I tell you!"

The Rarfell nodded and their ossane slowed. As Urith expected, the armed scouts drew closer on the narrow trail. Urith and Parca kept trying to avoid the branches while expecting the swing of a Borr's weapon striking them. Out of the corner of his eye, the Esterblud noticed a scout pulling a spear from behind his back. A glimpse to the other side showed Urith the enemy's mount; the creature's bulbus head near enough for him to touch.

"Now!" Urith yelled out.

Instantly, the warrior swung back with the Clovel Sword while aiming neck high. The blade cut into the scout's neck.

Parca hesitated, then followed the order. Despite the pain in his shoulder, he jerked back on the reins, which turned their ossane in front of the oncoming enemy who threw his spear. It missed them as the Borr's animal careened into Parca's. Urith reached out and grabbed the enemy by his robe with one arm. The momentum of the move and his weight forced the enemy to the ground, where the two men rolled away. Urith sprung to his feet, his sword immediately cut through the man's chest. The action caused Urith to clutch at his ribs but he kept moving as grab the enemy's ossane by the reins. By the time Urith got on the mount, Parca rode away.

As the warrior spurred his stolen ossane, more scouts coming down the trail hurried after him. Urith followed Parca, then took a hard turn in front of the oncoming Borrs. As he expected, the riders followed him. Urith used the thick vegetation to his advantage, weaving in between trees and brush until he fell out of sight. The Esterblud pushed his ossane into a formation of spiny *Icarcal* trees, then followed the slope of the land as it led down.

Urith avoided the worst of the unfamiliar terrain while his enemy remained close enough to hear. Using the mountains that broke out occasionally from the heavy forest to ensure his direction, he came to another fork in the barely seen trail. The Esterblud followed a path that he expected his comrades were heading. After pushing his mount through a dense area of vines and *wstinga* brush, he brought the ossane to a stop behind the thickest of the blue green thorny barrier. Almost immediately, Urith heard the galloping of several ossanes draw closer. They slowed, but the Borrs remained out of sight. He heard a voice telling the group to split up.

Urith waited, trying to see his opponents amid the brush as they drew closer. He pulled his shield off his back and slid his forearm through the straps. Hunched down in his saddle as two riders passed his position, the Esterblud waited, then spurred his mount back through the brush. He came out to follow them. When the men slowed, their attention focused upon finding signs of his tracks, Urith sped up. They failed to detect his oncoming charge toward them until the last moment. The scout closest to the warrior looked around just as Urith swung out his shield. The force of the blow into the man's head sent the leather helmet flying. With his sword in the other hand, Urith sliced into the back of his enemy on the other side of his ossane while he passed. When Urith halted and looked back, the enemy's mounts no longer had riders in their saddles.

Urith turned back around and hurried back to the enemy's ossanes. Only one of the Borrs lying on the ground moved. The Esterblud gathered the reins of the ossane's reins, then he tied them to his saddle. He trotted away, looking for a trail toward the mountains.

~~~

Darrca finally slowed when Hera told her they were coming to a river. While the terrain looked different from what he remembered, he noticed the large boulder, which was nearly hidden now by crawling vines. He told her to stop by the rock. Hera pointed to the partially obscured symbol on the face.
~~~

"My brother and I engraved the picture of an erba there. We'll go to a bridge where we can get on the road to the mountains."

Darrca looked at the engraving, smiling at the rudimentary work, which appeared nothing like the shaggy-haired beast of burden. She heard water rushing nearby.

"We need to stop for Parca," Esart interrupted as he pulled by their side. His ossane was limping badly.

Darrca and Hera looked back to see the Rarfell fighter struggling to keep upright in his saddle as he finally caught up with the others. A bloodstain covered his shoulder. Then Hera recognized Urith was missing.

"What happened to your partner?"

Parca explained, and Hera glared at Esart. He avoided berating the fighter for not slowing down to help in the fight.

"Cursed *brgensoc* Esterblud! He'll never find us now. We can't wait for him. The Gallaeci can't be that far behind us."

"I'm not sure about that," Parca replied as he gingerly checked his wound. "It looked like they followed him when he broke away. I can't be sure, but I've not seen any Borrs following."

Esart slid off the wounded ossane and went over to Parca's. "My ossane won't make it much farther. Slide back and you can lean on me. We'll continue on this one."

"What about Urith?" Durta spoke up.

Esart pulled himself on the saddle while Hera pulled the ossane around to look at the young man.

"Nothing we can do. He took the pressure off by leading the Borrs away. He knows we're overloaded and can't outrun anyone. I suspect he intends to follow us once he loses his pursuers in the forest."

"That's the hope anyway," Darrca agreed. "We must continue on toward the mountains."

"Yes, the Borrs can't find us once we get into the rocky terrain to cover our path. Let's find that bridge before the Borrs do." Hera spurred the ossane forward.

Mekan patted Dutra on his shoulder as they followed. Esart felt his brother put an arm on his shoulder and the two men hurried after the others.

The group reached the bridge; forcing them to slide off their ossanes to cross the moss-covered rickety structure. Several areas of the planking were missing, but highland *starkts* dropping showed them that shepherds still used the structure. Rushing water cutting through the V-shaped canyon below created a mist which covered the structure.

"We should destroy this bridge," Hera stated as he trudged in the lead. Esart left Parca on the ossane when they crossed. "Curse my hands!"

"You need time to heal. But I'll I can do it." Esart stated.

"No, we don't have the luxury of time. The Borrs might arrive at any moment. The next bridge is only a half-day downstream."

"If you think that's best, then let's continue on," Darrca quickly agreed as she followed Hera. "Perhaps we can trade the shepherds for food and drink on the way?"

"I recommend we avoid everyone. You're the last chance for Rarfell to survive as we know it. Phillo will kill anyone for the information on your whereabouts. Once we get out into the open, we're exposed. That means we can't slow down until we reach the mountains." Hera kept probing the wood planks with his boot before he moved forward.

Darrca frowned, silently chastising herself for not thinking about such things. She looked at the twin peaks in the distance, not even sure how far away they were. Her inexperience in traveling, combined with her uncertainty in leading her people, hit her with a wave of frustration. In her upbringing, Darrca's father and mother treated her as a prize for the next king of Rarfell. Exposed to the proper social customs and diplomatic niceties, Darrca rarely left the Cymeer. While she met many advisors, teaching her about the requirements of being a ruler was never a consideration. The only reason that the woman learned to handle a dagger was to impress her father. Her ability carried the added benefit to bring those around the king into her confidence as her husband's health declined. Still, all major decisions rested with her husband.

That's not happening again, she vowed.

"Can Parca make it to the mountains?"

"It doesn't appear the arrow went into his lung. Either way, he'll have to make it. We won't get there for another sunrise. Our mounts can't take such a hard ride with two riders. We'll need to walk part of the way for them to rest."

After they crossed the bridge, Hera focused his attention on the surrounding terrain. Esart stepped next to him.

"We should travel in a line and keep the ossanes in the middle of the trail," Esart recommended. "It makes it harder for them to determine how many of us went this way."

"That's a good idea." Hera agreed, then looked up. "Next time, you don't rely on an Esterblud to cover our rear or to help Parca."

Esart watched him turn away. Then the guard got on his ossane with his brother.

"Don't let it get to you. Next time, you'll know what to do." Parca grimaced as he adjusted himself behind the saddle.

"Cursed Esterblud!" Esart dug his heels into the flanks of their mount.

~~~

Yartha and his remaining scouts found the body of one scout and his badly injured companion not long after Urith attacked them. A foul expression covered the man's face. He recognized Phillo would put the blame on him and the scouts he led. The Gallaeci leader glanced over at one man. Arram carried the scars of a battle-hardened bandit and he came from the same tribe as Yartha.

"We should forget the Esterblud and go after the others," Arram said, then spit on the ground as he rose from looking at the injured Borr.

"Yes, Phillo wants Darrca," Yartha agreed with a growl. "But I want Urith skinned alive."

He pointed to the youngest rider in the group.

"You go back to Phillo and tell him we will catch our enemy when they break out on the open highlands. He can meet us there."

The young bandit's eyes widened at the thought of informing their leader of the bad news.

"Tell them we have a blood trail in the vegetation that we're following. Inform him we're being cautious so avoid killing the queen by accident in this dense forest. We're keeping close to catch on the other in the open terrain."

The rider nodded and reluctantly spurred his ossane back along the trail.

"That should help keep us from Phillo's wrath for a while," Yartha told Arram.

"What about our wounded man?"

"Kill him and let him explain his failure to Facarm. Come on, we'll pick up the trail of the queen. One thing I know about that Esterblud. His weakness is a pretty face. He'll double back to find them. Then I'll have my revenge."
~~~

Arram went over to the barely conscious man on the ground. He pulled his spear from a belt that hung over his back and thrust the tip into the man's heart. He slid his weapon back into the belt before walking back to his ossane. Arram remembered drinking with the dead man frequently.

It's too bad, he thought as he got on his ossane and hurried to catch the others.

After quickly picking up the path Hera took, the Gallaeci leader pushed his ossane through the forest quickly. As his men hurried along, the only sound was the panting breath of the mounts mixed with the clanging of weapons and the thundering pounding of the cloven hooves. They reached the bridge and slowed to a halt. Yartha scanned the area, but no human was in sight. The vegetation thinned away ahead of them, with the forest turning into a highland plain. One side of the path across from them held a pile of rotten cut timbers. It appeared someone planned on replacing the dilapidated bridge at some point.

Then, Yartha noticed the dust floating in the air far down the path, almost on the horizon.

"It could be them," Arram's gravelly voice agreed with his leader's thoughts.

"Well, their ossanes can't outrun ours. They're too far away to reach safety now." Yartha sent his best tracker across first to ride ahead pick up his prey's trail.

"I want them by nightfall, so stay close and we'll catch up with you."

As he watched the dust ahead, the scout started across the bridge. When the mount reached the midpoint of the bridge, the Borrs heard a yell from the other side of the river edge. Suddenly, Urith and the three ossanes pulled away from behind the pile of timbers. A rope suddenly sprung up. Attached to one ossane, the other end of the rope cut through the worn-out planks like a knife. A yell erupted from the Borr sitting on his mount in the middle of the bridge which suddenly wobbled around him. A middle support timber suddenly jumped out, then followed the rope that pulled it along the path. When it slowed to a stop, the bridge finally collapsed. The scream of the ossane joined with its rider as both fell amid the falling timbers into the water below.

After watching their comrade die before them, they looked across the river, where Urith slid off his ossane and untied the rope. He climbed back on his ossane and started following the Rarfell riders ahead of him. The Esterblud didn't look back at Yartha, who furiously screamed the terrible revenge he would inflict on Urith.

~~~

Parca was barely conscious when the trio of ossanes finally came to a rest as the sun finally set in the east. During their push toward the mountains, Esart recognized his brother's steadily weakening condition. In the dim light that remained, the Rarfell Guard helped Parca down and glanced over his wound. The gray flesh around the wound made a crackling sound when pressed. Esart never saw such a wound turn infected so quickly. He called over the others, who looked it over. Hera's somber expression revealed he'd seen such an injury before. He sniffed the area around the wound. Hera pulled away from the stench.

"Lay him down so he can sleep," Hera told Parca. Then he ordered the others to get their bags. "We'll keep the saddles on the ossanes so we can quickly leave." He looked at Darrca.

"We can't have a fire in this open area. I'll take the first watch."
~~~

"I'll help with the watch," the queen stated, then joined Mekan and Dutra to pull off the bags and blankets.

Hera waved Esart over to him.

"Your brother has blood stink. I've seen it one time before," he explained. Hera's expression betrayed his thoughts.

"There must be something we can do!" Esart insisted.

"If we had moss, we might try it, but the infection is deep inside of his chest. I know of nothing we can do. It's up to the Fates." He placed his hand on Esart's shoulder. The guard shrugged it away and went back to his brother.

Mekan came to Hera after watching and overhearing the conversation. She handed him a bag of heathmead. He thanked her and pulled off the stopper. After taking a deep breath, he drank deeply.

As the group sat in the moonlight coming from the two half-moons, they quietly ate the jerky meat. Dutra was the first to hear the hoofbeats coming from the trail. He wanted to say something when Hera whispered out.

"Quiet!"

The rhythmic trotting sound slowed, then came to a stop. Parca and Hera rose with swords in their hands, while everyone kept looking toward the last sound. The night noises from the insects stopped. In the deathly stillness around them, the night weighed on the group. Hera pointed to the other side of the camp and Parca quietly stepped over. He looked for movement in the shadowed landscape.

"You need to work on guarding your camp, Hera," Urith's voice came to them from the darkness behind the group. He stepped into view under the moonlight with his sneer grin.

"And I thought you were dead," the Rarfell Guard grumbled as he sheathed his sword.

"Not hardly, but I gave you some extra time." Urith kneeled down at Parca's side with a groan. His careful movement showed his chest pain remained.

Esart joined them and explained his sleeping brother's condition. Urith nodded, then grimaced when he rose.

"Yes, I've seen it as well. A friend died this way after a spear got him." He looked over at Dutra.

"Go to the trail and bring in the ossanes I have left there. Tie them with the others," he ordered. Urith turned back to Esart. "Maybe one of the bags on the Borr's ossanes has dried moss."

The young man hurried away. Urith watched him for a moment, then turned back to the others.

"I saw you leaving the bridge when I arrived. I knew I didn't have much time, so I improvised." He explained what he did to slow the Gallaeci. Urith noticed Hera and Esart glance at each other.

"Yartha got to the bridge while I waited. I think he'll follow me to the underworld now," the Esterblud grunted with satisfaction. "I don't know how long it'll be before they pick up our trail again."

"Even at full gallop, they can't reach us for a day," Hera told him. "We should get sleep and make it to the main pass before the Borrs can track us down. Still, I didn't like how the clouds hung over the area. I suspect we may encounter snow."

"That's not good. I guess we'll find out when we get there." Urith looked over at Dutra, who came back with the three ossanes. "And we have two more mounts."

Mekan got up and joined Dutra to help unpack the mounts.

"Did anyone else get hurt?" Urith asked. He glanced at Darrca, who remained quiet. She shook her head.

"I saw no tracks of wagons. Are there any villages this way?" Urith asked Hera.

"No, it's a path really only used by the herders. After we get into the mountains, one trail leads over the pass into Cahmais. It splits off, and another trail goes to an abandoned temple. Few people even know about that place."

"That temple has possibilities." The Esterblud took a bag that Dutra handed him.

"Do you want to take the first watch?"

The young man eagerly nodded at the idea, then Urith glanced over at Hera. The Rarfell leader scowled at him.

"If Dutra takes the first, then I can take the next one and you and Esart can decide who gets the last one." The Esterblud continued laying out the schedule.

"Are you taking charge?" Darrca interjected when she noticed Hera's reaction. "I already told Hera that I'll take a watch as well."

"A queen doing the warrior's watch! Now that's something I'll tell the skalds." Urith's face brightened in jest. Darrca remained unimpressed, her scowled deepened.

"I suppose it appears I'm taking control," the warrior finally conceded. "I thought using Dutra as a lookout provides good experience for him. Everyone needs rest considering the ride we'll have starting in the morning."

"It makes sense," Hera agreed. "But I want to know what you're planning from now on. You're too willing to go off on your own."

Urith looked at Darrca, who nodded in agreement. He fought the urge to point out their failed plan led them into this highland open area. It made them sitting ducks for an overwhelming number of fighters coming after them.

"Fair enough. Considering we can't double back into the forest from here, I'll give you a pleasant surprise. I think I can lead the Borrs away from you."

Urith searched through the bag and pulled out a piece of dried meat. He sniffed it, then took a bite. The warrior waited for a response, but an uneasy quiet settled over the campsite.

"What are you planning?" Mekan spoke for the others.

"Yartha is the key. I've figured out that he's wrapped up his pride in destroying me. I'm going to give him the chance."

"But Phillo leads the Borrs," Darrca pointed out. "He wants me."

Urith smiled at her.

"Yes, but he made the mistake of letting Yartha lead his scouts. Now, let me lay out a plan for you."

~~~

Phillo and his men arrived at the Gallaeci camp long after dark. Yartha greeted him, noticing the large man's fury looked ready to explode.

"You've still not caught them. Why have you stopped for the night?"

Yartha frowned, then nodded to the lathered ossane that Phillo rode.

"Walking back to Cymeer is ill-advised. According to those who know the area, there is only one path leading to Cahmais. They will not make good time. When we saw the clouds over the mountains as the sun set, we knew the Fates were on our side. Arrem believes snow will cover the mountain pass before we arrive."

The man's explanation calmed Phillo, who grunted when he glanced at Arrem. The Borr nodded agreement with Yartha, who handed Phillo a bag of heathmead.
~~~

"Very well, but I want us riding before the sun rises. With an open plain, they can't hide." The Borr leader took a deep drink, then slid off his mount.

As he went to the fire, two of the men quickly stripped his ossane of the saddle and blankets. They placed fresh blankets from another ossane on the ground where Phillo would sleep. The leader leaned back against his saddle after rejecting the dried meat offered to him. His attention went back to Yartha.

"You lost two men today, and you failed to encircle this Rarfell group."

Yartha glanced over at the young scout who told Phillo. The man avoided looking at him.

"They had a guard posted who must have heard the movement in the forest. The volley of arrows coming into their camp sent them scattering. You saw the undergrowth. We could have double the men and still not trapped them." He replied carefully. "At a fork in the path, one of them stayed behind and ambushed our men. He's the one who's the most dangerous in their group."

Phillo nodded.

"The Esterblud. Are they following him?"

"No, I believe he's on his own, trying to protect them." Yartha continued to stare at the young scout.

My opportunity to settle the score will come!

Phillo noticed Yartha's focus, and he smiled to himself.

"Then, I want you and your men to find them, then ensure they're trapped or cut off from the trail to Cahmais. After that, you'll wait for the rest of our men. Don't disappoint me a third time."

He watched Yartha walk away, then took another drink from his bladder. Since he met Yartha, Phillo believed the man held promise. He believed they held similar personality traits of fierce dedication to achieve their goals. Phillo held no illusions about fatherhood or raising children. Those women he bred meant nothing more than offspring for him to turn into dedicated fighters for Facarm. Those who failed to meet his expectations would die, just like Yartha should he not catch Queen Darrca.

~~~

Just before the sun rose, Esart heard a deep groan of pain which brought him out of a light sleep. He rolled over to find Parca taking his last breaths. His brother continued to worsen during the night and Esart recognized the Fates were against Parca. While the Rarfell man seldom went to the temples, he prayed Parca would meet their ancestors in Haligulf.

When the last of the Rarfell holdouts woke that morning, they found Esart on his knees, silently covering his brother's body with a blanket. They gathered around the scene while Hera stood next to the grieving man. He told him they needed to leave. Esart appeared not to hear him. Darrca stood on the other side and placed her hand on his shoulder.

"I know nothing I can say will help you, but everyone knows the bravery that Parca showed."

"I go to the temple this morning. Let's place your brother on an ossane. I give you my oath to burn the body in the funerary pit and I will say a prayer for his travel to Haligulf." Urith kneeled across from Esart.

The Rarfell Guard looked over before he finally nodded.

"He would like that. I thank you for my family."

Esart lifted the man's body with the help of Urith and they placed it over the saddle of an ossane. As the others quickly packed their mounts, Esart tied the body to the saddle. When Urith came back with his blanket and weapons, the Rarfell Guard stopped him.
~~~

"I still say your plan will only get you killed, but I swear to the gods that the skalds will know of this honorable thing you do."

Urith's expression turned foul at the comment.

"Don't go too far. I don't follow a path worthy of such honor. My grief hasn't left me. I still find solace when my blade cuts into a body, and I feel the warmth of my enemy's blood."

He turned away as Esart stood dumbfounded by the admission.

Urith tied off his bags and bedroll before getting on his ossane. He took ossane's reins that Esart held. Then Urith slowly set off for the trail to the mountains. Mekan and Dutra were already on their mount. She frowned when Urith paid no attention to them as he passed them. Instead, he was staring at the cloud covered mountains.

Hera stepped next to Esart, telling him to take the extra ossane. When Hera got on the mount with Queen Darrca, she watched the Esterblud. She overheard the conversation, which told her even more about the scarred man.

"If the weather holds, we'll get to the pass by midday," Hera's voice interrupted her thoughts. He dug his heels into the mount and soon joined the group.

"Do you think this idea will work?" The queen asked Hera quietly.

The man in front of her shrugged.

"Perhaps if we can show just one path. If you get away to safety, then it's worth a try. You heard Mekan agree Yartha carries a grudge against Urith. I believe both men want an ultimate battle."

"Why? Is this his wish to die in battle?" She watched as the ossane carrying Esart passed them. The Rarfell Guard pulled next to Urith's mount as Hera shook his head at her question.

"From what I know about the Esterbluds, Urith is giving himself a chance at vengeance. You saw how he kept sharpening his sword as he outlined the idea of becoming bait for the Borrs." He told her about Yartha and Urith's fight in the tavern when they met.

"My guess is Urith trusted the Gallaeci after their fight in the tavern. Now, he wants to finish that fight in the tavern. Yartha betrayed us. I put him in the Cymeer Company to fight for the Rarfell cause. I'd cut that traitor's heart out if I get the chance."

"All of us want the Borrs strung up along with their women," Darrca snapped. "But we're not trying to commit suicide. He's worth more alive than acting as bait."

Hera glanced back, but he didn't see her expression. Her worried tone bothered him. King Renni died protecting her and his kingdom.

I'm mistaken! She can't care for the Esterblud.

"Well, like many people, Urith can't let go of the treachery." He stated diplomatically. "But we have to get you to Cahmais. He's doing his part."

The woman sighed.

"I keep thinking about that. I pray to the gods that they give me a chance to remove Phillo's head without running to another kingdom. I'm heard things about King Asgurd which concern me."

"Yes, I suspect that he'll want to take advantage of a situation. In that regard, he's no different from Urith's king."

Hera heard Mekan's ossane snort near them. He looked over to see the woman listening intently to the conversation. She gave him an uncertain smile.

"I'm going to rely on your advice," the queen told Hera as she noticed eye contact between him and Mekan.

"While we rebuild our fighting force, I must persuade others to join us. I have no access to a treasury or valuables. That thought led me to the idea that we gather people who will fight from the villages as we go back to Cymeer."

Hera remained quiet at the thought. She sensed his hesitation.

"I want your advice, so speak freely with me."

"It is an option, perhaps a better plan," Hera conceded. "However, farmers and villagers seldom care to fight. They also have no goals to die for Haligulf. It'll take a skilled leader to bring them to your cause."

"You don't think I can do that?"

The Rarfell man fell quiet for a moment before speaking.

"I think you are unknown to your own people. Even King Renni did not travel among the Cyer or the Rarfell towns. Our kingdom never felt the need to grow beyond our tribal loyalties."

The queen nodded. She recognized the truth in his thoughts. Stuck between two larger kingdoms in a remote and mountainous region, Rarfell seldom felt the effects of warring armies pushing through or the invasions from the sea by raiders. The land was like its people, isolated and remote.

"Then I have much work to do," she told him with an air of confidence. "I appreciate your candor. Depending upon what we find in Cahmais, we must consider this option."

Ahead of the others, Urith quietly rode along. He glanced at the ominous darkening clouds, but any concerns fell by the wayside. He focused on the upcoming fight. Somewhere deep inside of him, he knew Yartha and he would meet again. Something in the back of his mind kept gnawing at him and the Esterblud recognized it. Once before, an enemy warrior bested him. He had the scar on his face to prove it. However, he learned from that experience. He could live with the idea of his first defeat coming at the hands of Kirowan, one of the greatest warriors of Vulthnal.

Yartha, on the other hand, was nothing more than a tavern brute. Raw and basically unskilled, yet he nearly defeated Urith twice. The intervention of others to finish the fight tore at the Esterblud's pride and he recognized it. The situation forced Urith to reconsider his skills. Since leaving Esterblud, the man no longer forced himself to train and improve his skills. It showed, and he vowed to correct that mistake as he took another glance at the sky.

"We're traveling into a storm," Esart's voice brought Urith out of his thoughts.

Urith nodded agreement, then looked back across the open plains. He noticed movement along a ridge far behind them. As he stared, he finally decided it was men on ossanes. Turning back to Esart, he asked how soon they would reach the slopes ahead.

"It'll be just after mid-day. Hopefully, before the snow comes."

"Let's hope the snow comes first," Urith grunted. "We'll have company by then."

Esart looked back and saw the Borrs. He got Hera's attention and pointed to the distant riders.

The column reached the narrow path winding upward into the clouds as the mist they expected soon turned to snow. However, it wasn't a heavy snow, just light flakes that swirled around the hooves of the ossanes.

"We will not lose them with this!" Hera groused as he wiped away the melting snow that ran down his face. "At least the Borrs can't see us anymore."

He waited for a response, but the building chill, along with the concern each rider felt about their pursuers, kept them quiet.

The column wound their way up along the rocky trail, reaching into the clouds which mixed with the swirling snow. After a while, the snow came down hard. Aside from the swirling white around them, their view only showed them the few plants which clung along the edge of the trail or the broken rock. Their pace slowed down to a crawl, with only the sound coming from the ossanes' clomping hooves and the metallic clang of their weapons and supplies.

Even with the heavy quilted undergarment and woolen tunic that he wore, Urith felt the cold pushing into his body from the chain mail he wore. Finally, he pulled a blanket over his upper body when the fog of his breath became visible. He glanced back to see the other riders were already using their blankets to keep warm.

Hera called for Urith to stop just after mid-day. Urith halted, then waited for the others to join him. Hera nodded toward a place between two large pillars which leaned back, almost oblivious to gravity.

"That is the trail that leads to the temple. Nobody really knows the name, so we call it *Aprarcau Racrwe*, Face in the Rock. Legend says it comes from the Guardians."

Urith scanned the ground around them and nodded.

"I'll stay here for a while and wait for the snow to cover your tracks. Once I hear them, I can follow that trail. It'll fool them into following these two ossanes as you and the others continue on to Cahmais."

"I still say you should go with us," Hera replied.

"I agree!" Darrca interjected. "A dead hero doesn't help Rarfell."

Urith grinned.

"You don't have much confidence in my ability. You forget I promised Esart. His brother must have prayers as his body burns in the temple. Good luck to you in Cahmais."

He turned the mount away. The others noticed Darrca's wounded expression.

"You're forgetting me," Dutra insisted as he jumped down from behind Mekan. He ran over to Urith's ossane.

"I can't monitor you and keep myself alive," The Esterblud shook his head.

"But you're planning on going to Haligulf. So will I." The boy pulled a short sword. His bravado, while holding the blanket over his head, nearly caused Urith to laugh.

"Dutra, go with the others." He told him.

"You promised to train me as a warrior. Is this how an Esterblud keeps his oath? There's no better place for me to learn than with you."

Urith avoided looking at the Rarfell riders, waiting on his reaction.

"Dutra, you're a fool!" Urith observed with a growl. He slid off his ossane, then glared at the boy.

"Get over here and take this ossane if you're coming with me."

Urith and Dutra pushed their ossanes hard. Dutra rode alone while Urith's ossane carried the body of Parca behind him. The young man asked why and the Esterblud grinned.

"My father, the noble warrior Uolven, taught me to confuse those who trail you. A good tracker can tell how many people are on a mount by certain signs. On this day, you get to play a queen!" The boy frowned at the statement and Urith laughed.

The riders rode side by side on the wide trail as they climbed the steep terrain to the temple. The snowfall lightened as they gain elevation. They soon came upon a streaming creek which ran next to the road. The riders moved to one side to avoid the ice covering part of their path. The frozen water spray came from the wind, which whipped around on the upward turns of the cobbled road. As they rounded a bend in the path, they saw the reason for the temple's name.

A large rock cliff held a giant face with oversized eyes which looked down upon them. A large stream of water spurted out of the open mouth, creating a strange waterfall. The Esterblud squinted at the path leading to the face in the stone.

"That's a good place to watch our enemy," Urith noted as he spurred his ossane through the remains of a gate.

The riders entered the massive temple courtyard. Their path circling next to a low dam holding a pond of water. Urith observed a stream of water pushing through the leaking cracks in the wall that stood at the height of his ossane. The flow of water rushed next to their road as it flowed down a hand-cut path. Two squat columns precariously lined the top of the dam wall with their white marble bases damaged from the fall of another fluted column.

Entering the massive circular courtyard which looped around the nearly frozen pond, the riders paused at the sight of the water pouring down from the open mouth of the giant face. The stream landed into a green tinged pond.

Standing on the outside of the courtyard were stone columns and remains of angled roofs of dark slate jumbled rumble into piles and covered with snow. A thick wall still held a boulder which tumbled from the cliff above. The stone matched other rocks, which must have come down when the land shook at one time. No building appeared intact inside the temple complex. Several of the structures made of wood had partial walls standing several persons tall, but their timbered frames only provided an outline to the once grand façade where the priests once worshipped.

Urith followed the courtyard path to an elevated platform which looked over the pond. The altar to the gods held a firepit, which he expected. However, he didn't see wood to start a fire. The Esterblud silently berated his stupidity.

"We won't be making a fire for the body until we find dry wood! We don't have time for that right now."

"At least we have water to hold out," Durta piped up.

"Our fight will not last long enough to worry about that when the Borrs dismount and hunt for us on foot," Urith growled.

As the warrior looked around, he noticed what Dutra was looking at. The small lake below them looked out over the valley. While snow and clouds covered the area, their perch showed him the road leading into the complex. A smile came to his face.

"Dutra, perhaps we have a fighting chance. You help me unload the body, then I want you to keep watch here for the Borrs," he tilted his head toward the valley. "Once you see them, come running to me."

The young man nodded, then helped Urith put Parca's corpse next to the firepit. Urith took the reins of both ossanes.

"Don't fail me in this task I give you. I've got work to do," the warrior told the boy as he climbed on his mount.

He galloped away to the dam below while Dutra stood watch over the path to the temple.

~~~

Yartha slowed his ossane at the fork to the temple. He waited for Arrum, who was coming back from the main path ahead. Only his tracks showed in the fresh snow. However, the man recommended they continue on his path.

"But the tracks lead up there," Yartha insisted.

The scout glanced over and nodded.

"They split up. See how the one ossane's prints aren't weighed down while the other is? Only one person is riding on that mount." The Borr slid off the ossane and walked to the multiple sets of prints. "They waited for the snow to fill in the main trail and they want us to follow that path toward the mountain. The other path shows two mounts, one small rider given the prints."

"Well?" Phillo rode up.

Yartha told him the news about the ossanes splitting up.

"Where does that path lead?" Phillo's eyes narrowed as he surveyed the tracks.

"I'm not sure," Arrum told him. "I've heard stories of Guardian priests on this mountain. Seeing those weathered stones, I'm guessing it's a way to their temple."

The Borr leader smiled.
~~~

"But of course. That explains why one ossane carries less weight. My little pet would never ride with another person. She's trying to play me for a fool." He looked around. "She sends the Esterblud and others on to Cahmais. Then she stays here with her remaining guards to rise the people of Rarfell against me."

He turned his mount to the mountain.

"We'll go to the temple and I'll enjoy myself while killing her slowly."

"I'll take the other path and follow that Esterblud and kill him before he gets to Cahmais." Yartha turned to follow the others.

Phillo stopped him.

"You must learn how people work, my young friend. The Esterblud will never enter the lands of his enemy. That's why he spoke about the idea when you were with him. You told me he lives by a warrior code which means will never abandon the queen. She's convinced her guards to continue on to Cahmais."

The leader's satisfied smile bothered Yartha when he turned his mount back. He wasn't as sure as his leader. However, the idea of killing Urith filled Yartha with a grim determination.

"You come with me. I'll let you repay him for escaping." Phillo ordered as he turned toward the snowy path leading to the temple.

~~~

As the Borrs rode to the temple, the rest of the Rarfell group sat on their ossanes not far away. They looked over the only trail to Cahmais, which no longer existed. Instead, they looked at exposed rock covering a deep gash which cut into the mountainside. Over the course of the latest Wyrnstrap, the
~~~

heavy snow on the top of the mountain let loose an avalanche, which swept down to leave a wide chasm. On the other side, they saw where the path continued their only escape route.

"If the Galleaci don't follow Urith, we are dying here," Hera stated the obvious. "I suggest everyone prepare their weapons."

"There's no place to defend ourselves here," Esart pointed out as he scanned the steep incline on both sides of them.

"Then we turn back." Darrca's voice carried a hint of relief. "There were places we rode by which can provide some defense."

"Yes, we have the advantage of a narrow road," Hera tried to sound optimistic, despite knowing the enemy had bows and arrows.

After making a careful turn, Hera and the others slowly began their trip back to the fork in the trail. The snow lightened as they followed their tracks. He heard Mekan catch Darrca's attention. When he glanced back, the Rarfell warrior saw Mekan hand the queen a short sword.

The two women exchanged a determined look, and Darrca thanked her. She slid the scabbard into her belt next to the daggers that Urith gave her. Mekan pulled another sword from the rolled blanket behind her saddle and hoisted the leather strap over his shoulder. She left a spear inside the blanket.

After rounding the second bend, Hera stopped. He noticed the hoof tracks from the Borr scout who returned to the main body of their pursuers.

"It looks like they took the bait," he spurred the mount forward.

"What's next?" Mekan asked.

"We hurry past and head back down the mountain. With luck, the snow will stop, and we can get back to the highlands." He frowned at the thought. Hera recognized the decision, still left them exposed once the Borr bandits finished killing Urith and Dutra.

"We can't outrun them." Darrca told him from behind.

"Quiet!" Esart hissed.

"What's that sound?"

A growing roar echoed above them. Instantly, they feared an avalanche was coming their direction. The riders hurriedly pulled their mounts close against the cut rock next to their path. Tension filled them as the roaring sound drew closer. Then, the noise moved in front of them as the ossanes became difficult to control with their whinnying and stomping. However, the cause remained out of their sight.

After the sound finally faded away, the riders cautiously pulled their ossanes back on the trail. They rode ahead until they came near the twin pillars. To their astonishment, the one pillar was missing, and its stone twin lay across the trail, split apart. A dead ossane lay next to the pillar while the land over the area held no snow. In its place, a black muck covered the path and the trail leading up to the Guardian Face in the mountain.

~~

"They're coming!"

The breathless announcement from Dutra as he came running. Urith finished tying off a rope to the saddle of an ossane. The Esterblud glanced down the trail as the column of Gallaeci trotted toward their position by the dam.

"Get on this ossane," Urith ordered. "When I tell you, I want you to put your heels into your mount like a *Clovel* is coming after you. Understand?"

With a nod, the young man climbed aboard the animal while Urith hurried to get on the other ossane. He'd already tied his mount to the column, precariously perched on top of the dam.

"Now!" Urith told him as he dug his heels into the ossane.

Instantly, the two ropes pulled taught from the top of the heavy column of stone. The ossanes snorted and slipped on the snow-covered cobblestone while their riders kept spurring them forward. As the mounts strained, Urith looked back to see the Borrs moving closer. He guessed well over twenty of the thugs approached. Phillo's armor stood out in the distance and the Esterblud noticed Yartha following close behind. As Urith dug his heels into the flanks of his ossane, he glanced over at the boy next to him, who wore no armor.

We won't last long!

Above him, Urith finally felt movement as the column inched over. He reached back and slapped his mount on the hip. He encouraged the ossane forward while the animal grunted in protest, then it strained against the rope. Dutra's ossane lurched forward at the same time, and the platform under the pillar cracked. The animals pulled harder when they felt the movement, when gravity eased their burden. The falling stone came down against the other column laying across the dam as the two mounts raced away, their broken ropes dragging behind.

After several paces, Urith halted his mount and looked back. Anger and frustration filled his face. He heard the grinding snap of stone, but the barrier holding back the water remained standing. He stared at the dam, willing it to fail.

"They're getting closer!" Dutra's voice rose.

Urith remained quiet. He simply pulled his shield from behind his back, then unsheathed his Clovel Sword.

"Do you remember the demigoddess Fedelm, whose image is on most of the Sacred Overlords temples?"

Staring at the onslaught of men coming, Dutra licked his dry lips and nodded. He glanced at the large warrior next to him, trying to emulate the steady, almost serene attitude his mentor carried.

"Since I was your age, I always wanted to meet her," Urith continued. He felt a growing sense of deadly calm that swept over him in situations like this.

"You know, a warrior goddess to hold in your arms while you drink in the afterlife isn't a bad goal. Besides, the skalds tell us that the heathmead tastes better in Haligulf," the Esterblud's sneer grin came out as he stared at the coming death.

"Fight like a cornered *brokko*. Claw their eyes and rip out their throats with your dying breath!" He told Dutra.

As he spoke, they heard a thunderous snap, which caused them to look over. A small stream of water broke from the crack in the dam wall. The pressure pushed the stream out further as the first Gallaeci arrived. Phillo slowed, crossing the column to bunch up behind him. Then, Yartha recognized Urith on the mount and he spurred his mount. Phillo joined him and they moved close to the canyon wall opposite of the dam. They passed through the stream of water, followed by more of their men.

Suddenly, another grinding sound rose, then the area around the center of the dam broke away. Large stones shot out, followed by a wall of water. The torrent cut through the column of Gallaeci fighters. Men and ossanes screams mixed with the rushing sound of the water. Phillo and those past the stream stopped and turned their mounts. They remained silent and dumbfounded by the amazing power of the temporary river heading down the valley.

Dutra and Urith watched in astonishment while their enemies flailed in the water, only to be flung against the rocks across from the trail. Ossanes and their riders futilely struggled in the surging green water as it swept them away. Flooding water filled across the narrow confines of the valley road, forcing the screaming Gallaeci riders along before they tumbled out of sight under the fast-moving stream. The boy stood in his saddle, suddenly bursting out in manic laughter at the scene. Urith glanced over and realized Dutra's reaction came from his idea that they might live.

However, the spectacle was short-lived when Phillo turned his attention away from the disaster behind him. He looked over to see the young man yelling in excitement. Enraged, Phillo spurred his mount while ordering the remaining men to follow him.

"Come on!" With shield and sword in hand, Urith steered his mount away. Dutra awkwardly forced his animal around and hurried after his mentor.

The two riders raced through the courtyard toward the altar platform. A quick glance back showed Urith the Borrs were gaining fast. He turned down an ancient street still clear of rubble. When he reached the narrow confines between sections of two broken stone buildings, the Esterblud halted.

"Into the rubble." he slid off his mount. Dutra dutifully followed, carrying a spear and a short sword.

They hurried up a stone wall which lay at an angle against the rest of the structure. The snow caused them the slip, but they made it to the top of the mound. Hearing the echoing sound of hooves as the Borrs entered the street, the men crouched out of sight. The Gallaeci riders headed straight for them as Urith and Dutra worked their way through the broken rooftop. They came to a stop behind a haphazard array of boulders which tumbled down on the temple from the cliff above.

Urith looked over the snow-covered area with a scowl. The remaining Borrs were already off their mounts. One group followed the footprints leading to his position. The other men came around another jumbled path, trying to cut off their prey's escape. The warrior pointed to a spot and motioned for Dutra to head toward the covered place.

When Urith arrived, one of the Gallaeci fighters was already waiting. The enemy jabbed at the Esterblud with a spear. Fortunately, Urith's quick reaction using his shield deflected the spear tip up into his arm. The warrior swung around with his sword, catching his opponent across the both outstretched arms. His blow cut through one forearm. As he left the screaming man, Urith kept moving while tugging at the spear tip still embedded in his chain mail sleeve. He quickly slipped around heavy piles of debris, finding stone stairs which led across the next level of broken buildings. The warrior paused long enough to remove the spear tip and look over his wound, which wasn't deep despite the pain.

When Dutra leaned next to the Esterblud, Urith gave him an encouraging grin he didn't feel. He turned to start up the stairs when he heard Dutra groan. He looked back to see the young man struggling to remove an arrow from his back. The Borr who shot him moved toward another position while drawing another arrow. Rage filled Urith, who pulled the injured boy past him.

"Get up those stairs and wait for me!"

The Esterblud sped across the open area between the piles of rubble. The crunch of his footsteps reaching his opponent, who quickly aimed at Urith. The Borr's arrow struck the warrior's shield with just a few paces separating the men. Urith continued forward as his enemy notched another arrow and drew back on his bow.

The Esterblud's downhill momentum and powerful arm slashed the Clovel Sword across the Gallaeci upper body. The blade cut through the leather armor and deep into the man's shoulder. Urith slipped on the snow, but he swept around with precision and his upward strike caught his enemy in the lower jaw. Blood splattered across both fighters as the Gallaeci fell with part of his face cut away.

Urith groaned as his chest suddenly felt on fire. His attack caused the injury from Yartha to return. The excruciating pain came from somewhere deep in the middle of his rib cage. Sucking the frigid mountain air, he hurried back to Dutra.

He found the wounded young man on his knees near the top of the stairs, which led out to another broken platform. As he stopped to catch his breath, Dutra's ashen face looked up at him.

"I can't get the arrow out," his voice trembled. "It hurts, but I'm not spitting blood."

With a grunt, Urith came around Dutra and looked over the injury. He paid no attention to the yelled instructions of Phillo to his men as they drew closer.

"It's in the meat of your shoulder next to your arm. Stay still!" He put his hand next to the shaft that protruded out of the cloth. "We have to hurry. Don't faint on me!"

The warrior probed with his finger to find the barbed tip hadn't entered the flesh too deep. Sliding his hand back, he quickly wrapped his hand around the shaft and pulled. Dutra shuddered and groaned, but he remained standing. Urith glanced around for a way to escape and noticed a slab above them. It held a crude tunnel within the rubble.

A movement among the ruins caught Urith's eye. Phillo and another Borr came into view and moved up the stairs. They looked down at their dead comrade. Urith grabbed Dutra by his tunic and lift him to his feet.

"I want you to wedge yourself in that space feet first. You'll be protected by arrows and it's too small for others to get in." Urith's face dripped sweat despite the cold as he gave the youth a spear. "I don't think they'll look for you. Just stab anyone in the face if they try to enter that place."

Before Dutra could respond, Urith pushed the boy on to the platform. The warrior's body trembled from the pain of his action. Dutra scrambled into the crevice while Urith hurried away. He picked his way past the stones and rubble, which continued to lead up toward the nearby cliff face. Eventually, he came to the edge of the building, which fell away into a deep jagged fissure in the ground below. When the ground shook in the ancient past, it appeared part of the temple complex fell into the long, wide fracture. On the other side, a few toppled structures remained.

A precarious bridge of debris covered in snow led to the other side of the fissure. As Urith gingerly tested rubble when he heard footsteps. He glanced to his side just in time to see Yartha rushing toward him. The Borr struck with his heavy mallet as Urith whirled around with his shield. The blow from the mallet slid away. The Esterblud's weak swing of his sword was easily deflected by Yartha's shield. As the two men exchanged blows, Urith awkwardly backed away on the rubble. His glance below showed the white of snow on the exposed pieces of columns and blocks of stone.

"Ready to die, Esterblud?"

Yartha slammed his mallet into Urith's shield, sending splinters of wood into the air. The Esterblud swung low with his sword and caught the Gallaeci near the ankle. However, it was a partial strike which caused Yartha to back away in pain. He quickly recovered.

"You need to learn how to fight," Urith growled as he noticed more of the Gallaeci approaching. He waited as Yartha cautiously moved toward him.

Behind Urith's adversary, Phillo and two of his men came to a stop. One of the Gallaeci looked for an angle to throw his spear.

"No!" Phillo told his man as he lifted back his skull-like helmet. "I want to see if Yartha can take that Esterblud."

Yartha glanced back when he heard Phillo. Fury filled his face, and the Borr pulled his dagger before he attacked Urith.

~~~

The unexpected flood coming down the mountain valley barely missed the Rarfell riders. Hera and Darrca forced the others to join them next to the cut stone on one side of the trail. They watched with concern and amazement as Urith's water trap overran the trail. Occasionally, the bodies of the Borr victims and their ossanes floated by before sliding down the cliff below. Esart pointed out the bodies of his enemies going by him. He counted them with growing delight.

"I don't see Urith or Dutra," Mekan stated with surprise. "I wonder if their bodies already went by?"

"No, the gods are with Urith!" Darrca's face lit up at her confident statement. "I didn't see Phillo either. They're at the temple. I know it."

"I don't know how we can," Hera told her as the water receded almost as quickly as it appeared.

"We have to try," Mekan suddenly agreed. "I must know Yartha is dead or I kill him."

Darrca caught the woman's implacable expression. While the queen only spoke with Mekan occasionally during
~~~

their journey, she recognized the unsettled bitterness buried behind the woman's eyes. Darrca briefly wondered if she was looking in a mirror.

"Hera, I have unfinished business at the temple. Now find a way up there."

The group traveled along the washed-out path, which soon turned treacherous with ice. Forced to dismount, the Rarfell riders walked along with their ossanes. They tried to avoid the quickly formed ice on wet sections of the road overrun by the flash flood. It wasn't long before they came upon the dead and injured Gallaeci. Esart hurried to the struggling men and took great pleasure in killing those who survived drowning. On the journey, Mekan came upon an ossane that survived. She struggled to get the skittish animal to follow them.

Hera was the first to see the broken remains of the dam as they rounded the bend leading to level land. The sight slowed them for a moment as they took in the sight.

"But how did this happen?" Esart hurried next to Hera and Darrca after finishing off the last injured Borr.

Hera shook his head, then spurred the mount on as the others followed. They came upon ossane prints in the snow along with the impression of two lines dragged behind. Hera jumped down for a closer inspection. Mekan directed her ossane toward the valley wall where she saw tracks on the snow

"I guess you're right about Urith," Hera conceded aloud as he crouched. He showed them a length of rope buried in the snow that was used to topple the column. "You can see where he and Dutra pulled down that stone." He rose; his eyes following the two sets of ossane prints leading through the courtyard.

"Looks like we have more Borrs following them," Mekan announced as she pointed to the line of tracks close to the valley wall.

She spurred her mount and followed the tracks. Hera hurried to get on the ossane with Darrca as Esart galloped past them to catch Mekan. Soon, they found the ossanes at the end of a street surrounded by rubble from the temple complex.

Immediately, they heard metal against metal, along with shouts and yells. Hera got down from the ossane while trying to get Darrca to stay behind.

"You're the ruler of Rarfell. We can't have you captured or killed."

Darrca paid no attention as she slid off the saddle. Without a word, the woman rushed toward the sounds of battle. A protesting Hera followed her as Esart and Mekan joined them. Finally, Hera gave up and struggled to pull his sword. He motioned Esart to follow one trail of tracks while he followed the other. Mekan and Darrca decided to follow Hera. It wasn't long before they came across the first injured Borr who was crouched down a few paces away. Hera carefully crept up on the enemy, who remained focused on staunching the bleeding coming from his stump. The Rarfell warrior quickly killed the wounded man with a swing of his sword, which sent the man's head rolling across the snow.

"It's easy to find Urith's path," Mekan told Darrca as they came out from behind a broken column. "You were correct about the gods favoring him."

"Yes, somehow I knew they must protect him," she agreed. "How else could he escape death so many times? I should have listened to the Esterblud. Now we need to wipe out the rest of these vermin."

"Let's find Phillo!"

Darrca stepped past Hera as he shook his hand from the burning pain in his thumb. His action caught Mekan's attention. However, before she could ask, the man turned and hurried to get ahead of the queen. She picked up her spear and followed.

On the other side of the fallen building, Esart heard the echo of metal striking wood along with a catcall from a voice he recognized. He rushed through the rock-strewn path toward the source of the sound. As he passed the corner, he found the open area in front of the crevice. Then, he saw Phillo and his men as they watched Urith and Yartha battle.

Esart attacked the three men as revenge overwhelmed any thought of caution. Unfortunately, they heard him coming. The two Borrs pulled in front of Phillo and took on the Rarfell guard. Esart threw his only spear, which failed to strike. The two Borrs met the onrushing Rarfell, which quickly turned into a bloody battle. Esart's skill over the other men was apparent. However, his need for revenge caused him to make the mistake of taking his opponents in the open area. The Borrs spread out around him, attacking him from behind when he went after one fighter. Much like the horuks, the Borrs slashed at their enemy, causing him to react against their attack.

Phillo glanced at the battle, then turned back to watch Yartha pounding his mallet into Urith's shield. He smiled when the Esterblud slipped on the ice, sending him to one knee and Yartha pressed his advantage. The Borr sliced Urith across the exposed area of his shield arm with his short sword. His blood flowed as the warrior swung out with the shield and caught Yartha in the leg with the wooden edge. The move forced the Borr to back away in pain.

When Hera rounded the corner of rubble, he saw Phillo with his back to him. He immediately went after the Borr leader. One of Phillo's men shouted a warning, and the leader turned. He stood impassively when Hera reached him. Hera's swing deflected off the Borr's mallet. When Phillo the move and he avoided the weapon.

Reassessing his attack, Hera backed away. Phillo smugly grinned.

"You're no match for me. Killing you won't take much time."

Esart yelled out a warning and Hera spun out of the way of a Borr fighter's blade that narrowly missed. Esart could provide no help since he remained locked together with the other fighter. Both men tried to gain the advantage as they grappled. Esart slammed his fist into his opponent's face. However, the action didn't weaken the man's grip. Instead, the Borr tried to gouge at Esart's eyes. Esart sought his dagger in his belt, when he suddenly felt a jab in his rib. The slicing pain spread as the Borr pulled away. Enemy's hand held Esart's dagger. A surprised disbelief filled the Rarfell's face as he fell to his knees. His killer slowly backed away with a satisfied smile.

A few paces away, Hera glanced over in time to see Esart fall and the Borr fighter with his back to him. Without hesitation, Hera sprinted over, leaving his two opponents. The Rarfell leader jammed his sword into the lower back of the Gallaeci who stood over Esart. The man fell next to Esart. Hera quickly turned back, expecting to meet Phillo and his last warrior. Instead, Phillo no longer appeared interested in him.

While the last fighter with Phill attacked Hera, his leader walked toward Darrca who came into view.

"My pet has returned!" Phillo mocked the queen.

She held Urith's daggers in each hand.

"You are dying today!" Her bitter voice caused the man to laugh.

"My little woman intends to hurt her new husband. Then, I must ready myself for battle." Phillo slid down the helmet, which had a partial mask which protected his nose and eyes. His head looked like a grinning skull.

Suddenly, Mekan stepped from behind the remains of a wall. She came to stand next to the queen with a spear in her hand.

"This gets better and better," the Borr brute flipped his heavy mallet easily in one hand. "I'll have two pets to play with when my men are through with your protectors." He glanced back at the fights occurring behind him.

"Don't worry, I'll only break your leg bones. Then you can lie beneath me while I rape you. I'll enjoy your screams. You'll beg for death!"

He strode toward the women, pulling his short sword.

On the rubble bridge, Urith's fight with Yartha left both men winded and bloody. Urith found himself cut off with his back against the rock face of the cliff overlooking the temple complex. Their fight pushed the men to a narrow strip of icy, snow-covered blocks of rock overlooking the deep crevice. Yartha rushed him and penned Urith's sword arm against the cold stone. Unable to retaliate when he slipped along the edge, Urith hung on with his other hand to keep from sliding down the rock face. Pressing his advantage, Yartha swung his mallet, which caught the Esterblud in the belly. When the Borr came around for another blow, Urith let loose of the wall and trapped Yartha's arm. The two men stood face to face, each unable to move without falling.

"I can see it in your face. You knew I would kill you," the Borr smirked. "A Borr is an actual warrior. You're just a noble who'll die like a peasant."

"You talk too much." Urith growled, then rammed his head into Yartha's nose.

Still hanging on, Yartha pulled down on the Esterblud, who slipped to one knee. Yartha grabbed for a dagger from his belt while the blood ran down from his nose.

Suddenly, Urith swung out with the pommel of his Clovel Sword. He struck Yartha in the crouch. As the Borr grunted and doubled over, the Esterblud slammed his head into the Borr's face again. The dagger in his enemy's hand dropped and banged off the stone.

Falling back and losing his grip, Yartha tried to grab Urith. However, the Borr's hands found only air. He yelled out and slid down into the crevice. Urith swung at the falling man with his sword. His blade cut through the man's arm. Yartha's screams continued until he fell out of sight into the darkness. Urith looked over the edge. He saw his enemy laying among the split rocks and snow. Yartha didn't move.

"Help the others!"

Dutra's voice carried over Urith's painful gasps for air. He looked across the crevice to see the young man come out from the rubble. He frantically pointed to the other end of the rubble bridge. Urith saw Hera and the last Borr fighter locked in a deadly struggle. Further away, he saw Phillo.

With a grim smile on his face, Phillo moved toward the women. As he drew close, Mekan suddenly stepped forward. Her attempt to stab him with the spear failed. The metal point glanced off his breastplate. Phillo swung around, his sword blade sliced at her, catching her in the upper arm. In practiced precision, he swung around with the mallet, striking her in the thigh. A hideous snap filled the air as the woman cried out in pain from the shattered bone. Mekan fell to the ground two paces away from Darrca.

"That's one pet down. Don't bother trying to leave. I'll come back for you," he growled. "Now it's time to care of a queen."

Phillo's last Borr fighter screamed as he died at the hands of Hera. The noise caught Phillo's attention briefly. He looked back at Hera, who was too far away to help Darrca.

"Now it's time to finish this!"

When Phillo turned back to Darrca, he glimpsed something flying at him. Instantly, pain filled his eye socket as one of Darrca's daggers struck, its blade sliced through his eye. Instantly, with the initial shock, the man cried out. Dropping his mallet, he frantically tried to pull on the dagger, which was stuck in the eyehole of his helmet. As he thrashed around, the large brute didn't see Darrca stepping closer to him.

"Time to fight me, you calward!" Her bone-chilling tone carried over his agonized groan.

The Borr leader blindly swung his sword, but his focus remained on trying to pull out the embedded dagger. Urith finally stepped away from the precarious ledge and hurried to the fight.

Urith and Hera came together a pace away and stopped as Darrca elegantly sidestepped the sword stroke of Phillo. The woman came in low and behind him. She sliced her dagger deep into the man's unarmored back thigh. The queen quickly backed away as he swung around, falling to a knee.

"Isn't that how the horuks do it?" The woman mocked him. "You promised me that fate, you worthless peasant!"

Dutra came next to Urith as he watched the queen. He noticed how much her expression of hate and revenge changed Darrca's attractive face. In her moment of triumph, the queen reminded him of the hideous *Iiloon* witches that terrified him when he first saw them on Cymeer's temple walls.

Phillo took another feeble swipe with his sword. Darrca swept in and stabbed her dagger between his chest armor at the neckline. The blade cut deep into his muscular neck. Shocked at his coming fate, he quit trying to pull the dagger out of his eye. His bloody hand sought his mallet on the ground.

"Look upon Queen Darrca. I'm the one who kills a so-called demi-god."

The woman grabbed the top of Phillo's helmet and drove her dagger through the other eye hole. The blade plunged into Phillo's brain. Instantly, the hulking body fell over while it quivered. Darrca stood over him for a while as the misty puffs of her breath mixed with the light snow which fell.

"I want his head on a pike and his scrotum made into a leather bag!" she told the onlookers quietly as she turned away to help Mekan.

~~~

Urith and Dutra cleaned and covered their injuries with the help of Darrca. Hera found two spears to make a crude splint for Mekan's leg. The woman grimaced and groan as Hera worked to secure the wooden shafts around her thigh. She cursed him under her breath several times. After he apologized again, she told him to shut his mouth.

"I'll survive! Just get it done," she growled. "I thought warriors knew how to put on a splint."

Mekan glanced up and saw Dutra came over to watch. He had a grin on his pale face.

"What are you smirking about?" Mekan lashed out.
~~~

"You just remind me of how Urith acts when he's in pain," he told her. Then he walked over to the crevice edge.

"Oh, don't you start," Mekan saw the suppressed smile on Urith's face as he joined them.

"I'm not saying anything," he replied as he glanced over at Dutra. "I'm sure you'll make him pay for the remark." His expression turned to reveal his concern. "You will have a painful ride on the back of an ossane with no *geju* root to chew on."

"Maybe we can rig a *trivis*?" Hera suggested. "Drag her behind an ossanes with a couple of long poles and blanket stretched between them. We can use what's left of the rope you have. It should make it easier on her."

Urith nodded agreement, then he noticed Darrca standing over the body of Phillo. Placing her foot on his head, she pulled out the daggers. The queen picked up the dead man's sword and cut his head off.

The Esterblud heard Dutra calling for him.

"On the way back to the ossanes, we'll look for something in the ruins that might work."

The Esterblud grimaced from the pain of his ribs as he walked over to the crevice edge where Dutra waited. He recognized the worry that filled the boy's face.

"He's not there!"

"What are you talking about?" Urith stared down into the darkened area. He immediately recognized what Dutra was talking about. Tracks lead away from where Yartha fell.

"The cursed snow must have let him live." Urith snorted as he pulled out his Clovel Sword. "You get back and help the others. I'm going to find out where that pitshog went."

He worked his way back on the rubble bridge, following the tracks from above as they went deeper into the crevice.

Eventually, he could no longer see the footprints. However, he realized the path might lead back to the ossanes. The Esterblud hurried back to the others. Hera and Dutra just lifted Mekan from the ground when he arrived. Urith had to catch his wind.

"Yartha is still alive. I think he's going to the ossanes. I'll try to cut him off." The warrior hurried away, but Darrca quickly caught him.

"Hey, you're in no shape to go alone," the queen told him.

"I'm not dead," he growled.

Darrca came next to him. "Don't argue! I'll go with you, Esterblud."

As quickly as they could follow the slippery path to the ossanes, they finally reached the street. Darrca noticed Yartha come out at the other end of the road, trying to get on one ossane. As he struggled to get on the mount, she warned Urith. Yartha galloped away before they could reach their ossanes. The Borr was out of sight when Urith steeled himself to lift his body over the back of the mount. His painful grunt caused Darrca to grab the reins, keeping him from going after Yartha.

"Leave him for the moment. We need your help here. I noticed he had trouble getting on the ossane with his injury. He can't run away any faster down that slick trail than we can. It was tough enough coming up that path," the queen reminded him. "Now you promised Esart that his brother's body would burn on the altar. We must do the same for Esart. Yartha can wait!"

The warrior glared at her. However, his anger faded when he realized she was correct. He stared down the valley trail as the snow still lightly fell.

"Alright fair queen, I understand. Since Hera is the only uninjured warrior left, you want him to trail Yartha. Is that it?"

Darrca patted his leg.

"Sometimes you can listen to others." Their eyes connected and he felt an emotion he thought lost.

"I'll try to remember that."

Hera and Dutra interrupted the moment as they approached carrying Mekan. After a quick explanation of Yartha's escape, Darrca sent Hera after Yartha. The man's reluctance was obvious as he kept glancing at Mekan.

"You'll do this for Mekan," the queen reminded him. "He's injured so you can catch him. Kill him before he can get more of the Borrs."

The Rarfell Guard turned to her. For a moment, she thought he might resist. Then he nodded.

"You stay safe. I expect he'll go to the closest village. He'll pay for what he's done."

"I'll bring the head of Phillo for your queen," Urith told Hera. "I wish I could join you."

Hera checked out the bags on the ossane. He avoided looking at Urith.

"I'll see that Yartha is yours." Hera took the reins from Darrca and rode away. Urith watched him for a moment, wondering what the man meant by his comment.

While Dutra and Urith went to get Esart's body, Darrca pulled a bag of heathmead from an ossane for Mekan. As the queen looked down the trail at Hera, who disappeared around the bend, she knew Mekan was staring at her.

"What are you thinking?" Darrca asked.

"You've changed since we first rode together," Mekan grimaced.

"I'm the queen. I have no choice. You're shivering, I'll get a blanket. Then we'll find a way to get you back to Cymeer."

"You should let Urith go back to Esterblud."

Darrca glanced down after she pulled a tied blanket from the back of the saddle.

"What makes you think he won't?"

"I've watched him and you as well. He'll follow you." Mekan leaned her head back in the snow.

"I don't know that such things should concern you. You wanted Yartha dead and Hera will do that for you now. Urith failed to kill him."

"Hera might not get him. His first responsibility is protecting you. Yartha is wily like a wild kuon. Fearsome with their large canines, but they hunt in packs like Borrs. You should let Urith hunt him, no matter where he goes."

They heard Urith's distant grousing at Dutra, which carried down in echoes from the rubble.

"I know you don't want Urith to leave. I noticed it in your eyes when he became the bait for Phillo."

Darrca crouched down by the injured woman. Her face remained coolly detached at the observation.

"I wonder why a farmer's daughter worries about this Esterblud. Did he promise you something that you can't get from Hera? You know he can't take back you to his homeland and settle down as a farmer. He's of noble blood and more suitable to my needs." The queen's tone was like the frost.

"He's a wanderer who needs a place where he uses his talents," Mekan replied, then suppressed a groan.

Darrca stood and dropped the still tied blanket next to the woman.

"Despite our shared experience, we're not of the same class or family. I will rule Rarfell. The kingdom needs warrior skills, and we have few warriors. Urith is useful and will lead my efforts to punish the Borrs. When we return to Cymeer, you will go back to your life. You should worry about keeping Hera should that broken leg turn you into a cripple." She turned away to gather the nearby ossanes.

Dutra and Urith placed Esart's body to Parca's in the pit. Then, they found a stash of dusty bluewood pressed under fallen roof timbers which they used. It took a while for them to start a fire, but after the flames leaped around the bodies; he taught the young boy the Esterblud chant for the dead. Darrca joined them and told Dutra to look for poles to create a device to drag Mekan behind the ossane. The youth hurried away, leaving the queen with Urith.

"I gave Mekan a blanket." She looked down at the washed-out road. "Your idea of using water nearly stranded you here until the next festival. It's a good thing that we came back."

Her smirk caused the Esterblud to sigh.

"I guess I'm never going to hear the end of that. A guy can't win with you around."

"No, not anymore," she agreed.

Chapter 8: Revenge and Retribution

Yartha finally reached a village called Arlar as the sun topped the trees of the next day. The small hamlet stood along a muddy creek at the fork of roads which led to Esterblud and back to Cymeer. With one broken arm in a crude sling he fashioned from a piece of leather, Yartha slowly entered Arlar. The round homes made of clay bricks and thatched roofs lined the road. He looked carefully at the few inhabitants who paid him little notice. The large trees at the crossroads cast their shadows over two rectangular building of more substance. The Gallaeci raids left the buildings as burned out husks.

When he reached the squat looking building that held a tavern, the Borr recognized the saddle markings of the Gallaeci on the ossanes hitched at a pole. He pulled his ossane next to the others and clumsily got off the mount. With his sardonic grin, Yartha walked into the tavern,

Yartha stopped in his tracks when he immediately recognized Hera sitting at the table in front of him. The Rarfell leader held a clay mug of heathmead in his hand. Behind the Borrs, a group of armed farmers stepped in behind him. One of them closed the door.

"I figured you would feel at home when you saw those ossanes outside. You're not from this land, so you don't know the quickest routes when someone follows you." Hera commented, then took a drink while the farmers quickly stripped the Borr of his weapons.

Yartha's eyes narrowed as he looked at the surrounding men.

"You think these unarmored peasants will run off the Borrs?"

"No, we have better plans for the Gallaeci." Hera stood. "I'll show you what will happen to the invaders."

He led the group through the building and out the back door. As they walked past a stand of smaller trees, they came upon an ancient yan-yew tree. Its massive branches extended out from the trunk high above their head. Dangling by their necks beneath the limbs were the remains of Borr fighters. The gathering flock of vensars were already pecking out the eyes of the corpses.

"My friends and I came into the village before dawn to wake your friends. We slit the throats of some men. The rest we hung here. Soon, we'll sell the Gallaeci wives and children as slaves to the Cahmais traders who come through. This will provide the repayment for your invasion."

Hera's lips curled into an evil smile.

"Once word spreads to the Gallaeci about how we treat our captives, they'll no longer insist on joining other families in Rarfell."

Hera drained the heathmead in the cup, then stepped closer to the larger man.

"We've learned from your brutal and underhanded tactics. At the end of the day, your people cannot win because there are more Cyer and Rarfell people living on our land. Farmers and peasants with their weapons can overwhelm your armored men with ambush when we travel to Cymeer. We will use our numbers to remove your invading tribe. Any Borr we find will die or suffer as slaves under the yoke of the Cahmais king."

Yartha looked around at the grim-faced men around him.

"If you're going to hang me, I think you forgot the rope." Yartha grimly joked.

Hera stepped closer. He broke the clay mug across Yartha's face. The Borr fell back as the several men took hold of him.

"Shut your mouth! You should know that I'm very tempted to flay you alive for what you've done to Mekan," the Rarfell leader's voice quivered with rage.

He nodded and one of the burly men behind the Borr held Yartha's head. Hera took the handle of the broken mug and cut across Yartha's face with the sharp edge. The Borr refused to yell out as the blood flowed down his cheek.

"You see, my hands are still useful. As I hung by my thumbs, I listened to every word you said. I know in detail about your people's plans. I made a vow when I escaped I would return and hang every Gallaeci. We enjoy watching you scum dangle and die a slow death by the noose."

"Then, get it over with!" Yartha sneered back.

Hera smiled.

"No, you'll not hang today. I have a better idea for you."

The men holding Yartha pushed him face down on the ground. Hera took the man's mallet and kneeled next to the prisoner.

"Hold his arm out," he ordered. A grim-faced man next to Hera laughed as he pulled out Yartha's uninjured arm.

"Your master tried to cripple Mekan. You will receive similar punishment." He told the struggling prisoner. Hera brought down the heavy weapon on Yartha's forearm. A sickening snap followed by the Borr's pain-filled howl filled the air. The men lifted the groaning man from the ground. After they forced him around the tavern, Hera stopped them in front of the ossanes. He pointed to an ossane that favored one leg.

"You can have my ossane since it came up lame in my hurry to reach you," Hera told him.

The group of men laughed and jeered as they forced the howling man onto the mount. As the pale faced Borr sat there, his one broken arm hung down. The man's other remained in the crude sling.

"As your dead Phillo liked to say, I'm giving you to the Fates," Hera announced. "We'll start you on the road to Esterblud. It's up to you to figure out how you survive. Too bad that I'll never know if you die before Urith gets to you."

Despite the agony he endured, Yartha understood.

"You're using me as bait to get rid of Urith." A bitter sneer filled his face.

One of farmers forced the leather reins into Yartha mouth. "I hope your teeth are strong. An injured ossane sometimes gets frisky and bucks to remove the rider."

The jovial men led the injured rider and lame animal to the road. As they taunted the Borr, Yartha saw Gallaeci woman and children tied to a tree at the edge of the village. With most of their clothes stolen, they tried to huddle despite their bound hands.

"Give my best to Caruun," Hera gloated as he slapped the rear of the ossane.

The mount trotted away as the groaning rider struggled to guide the animal along the rutted road.

~~~

Following Hera and Yartha's tracks in the snow, Urith dragged Mekan behind his ossane on the jury-rigged trivis. The progress was slow down the frozen mountain until they reached the highlands. However, Urith found creqweed after they reached a creek. The narcotic effect dulled the pain for Mekan while Darrca pressed them to increase their pace. As they rode along, the Esterblud kept finding his thoughts interrupted by the talkative queen. Mostly, she outlined her
~~~

future for the kingdom. As he listened to her plans, he understood the queen was looking for his acceptance, not his thoughts. Her firmness and commitment to the cause impressed him. However, there was a darkness she held he knew came from her experience with Phillo. He looked at the bag that held the dead man's head on her saddle.

At least you're now dealing with the underworld, you wretched cur!

Even in battle, dying at the hands of two women sent Phillo to the realm of Caruun. While women fought and died in the great battles of the past, the skalds never mentioned their ascent to the warrior's paradise called Haligulf. Even the battles fought and won by the great demi-goddess warriors of the past didn't mean their spirits traveled to Haligulf. Instead, their souls went to the Sky Realm among the gods. The logic of a paradise escaped him. Faith moved the realms, but not Urith. In his heart, the man always remained suspicious of skalds and their tales. It was fine to drink with such men and listen to the myths of the elder's great battles. He knew enough about people to realize stories handed down from each clan over the seasons slowly changed and transformed.

"Esterblud, are you not listening?" Darrca's voice brought him out of his thoughts.

"Just thinking about your plans," he lied.

"I saw you looking at the bag holding my enemy's head. Would you like to see the bag that holds his scrotum?"

There was amusement in her tone. He glanced over at the woman. His sneer smile was automatic.

"It's getting near dark; we should find a place to camp."

"Mekan says we're a short way from Arlar," Dutra spoke up from behind them as he walked beside Mekan's trivis. "Just around the bend ahead."

"Good, let's hope we can find a healer," Urith said.

When they reached the village, the sky was nearly black. The Esterblud left the group and carefully circled the village. He came across the hanging Borr bodies, nearly running into the bare foot of a dead man. Even in the growing darkness, he saw the tattoos on some of the bloated faces. Urith trotted back to the group and told them the news. Darrca led them into the village.

When the group came to a stop in front of the tavern, they heard a celebration going on inside the building. Urith and Darrca left Mekan and Dutra outside and went inside. The room was full of men and their families. The festive immediately ceased when the Rarfell people saw the large stranger in his Esterblud tunic. Immediately, Urith felt the hostile stares.

"Darrca" Hera pushed through the wall of people.

Suddenly, the atmosphere changed when he announced their queen's presence. Cheers rose from the farmers and merchants, many of whom had never seen Darrca. She smiled at the reception, her manner automatically turning stately and aloof. Hera led her through the gawking people who showered her with warm complements. Urith followed, forcing his way through.

When they reached a corner table, Queen Darrca turned and held up her hands for silence.

"People of Rarfell, tonight you've given me a great honor with your warm welcome. Know that the Cyer and the Rarfell people will remove the invaders who invade our lands. I only ask that you are ready for the coming fight that will require your sacrifice. Please continue your celebration while I speak with my advisors."

After basking in the cheers, Darrca took a seat while Hera pulled next to her. Urith sat across from them as Hera quickly explained how he took over the village with the help of local farmers. He told her of his plans to remove the Gallaeci village by village.

"Your idea is brilliant," the queen grew excited by the news. "I must admit that I did not know the people's love for me."

"Yes, well, the Borrs haven't made things easy for them." Hera glanced at Urith. "You can take advantage of their mistake."

"And we shall begin at first light. I expect every man in this village to swear allegiance to me. Then, I want every Cyr or Rarfell man and woman who can weld a sword or spear to rally around me. We will drive to Cymeer and take their land back." Darrca's eyes were alight with anticipation.

Hera hesitated, but smiled in agreement.

"I'll make the arrangements. Where's Mekan? I can take her to the village healer."

"Dutra's with her outside," Urith spoke up. "What about Yartha?"

Hera stared at the Esterblud.

"He got away when I went to several farmers to help me capture the Borrs in the village. Not to worry, he's on a lame ossane taking the road to Esterblud. He won't get far. Get some rest and follow him in the morning."

Urith, exhausted from the battle and trip, considered the idea, then nodded. Revenge carried a warrior only so far.

"Let's get help for Mekan."

Hera went to find accommodations for Darrca while Urith joined Dutra outside. The boy was holding a torch in his hand. Mekan came out of her light doze when he arrived. She smiled weakly at Urith as he kneeled by her.

"We're taking you to a healer here. The village has no Gallaeci to worry about."

"I won't be much good during your hunt for Yartha. Please kill him for all the pain he's inflicted."

"I will, but how did you know he got away from Hera?"

The woman grinned.

"Dutra already told me about the events of the village. He overheard the people in the tavern talking about the day. The little sneak looked in the tree for his body."

Urith placed his hand on the boy's shoulder and gave a reassuring squeeze. Hera and Darrca came out of the tavern with an old woman, who came down the step to look at Mekan.

"Take her to my place," the *mhoda* told him.

The small hut that Turun called her home barely held the group inside. Urith and Hera placed Mekan on a bed in the middle of the hut where Turun gave the injured woman the juice of *geju* root along with other herbs. It wasn't long before Mekan was asleep.

"I only need one of you to help me set her leg," the old healer said. "Then she'll need a place to stay for a while."

"That'll be me," Hera insisted. "Is she going to heal?"

The old woman shrugged her shoulders.

"The rest of you return in the morning. This woman needs time to sleep."

They left the hut and went back to the tavern, where Urith got a room for him and Dutra. The Esterblud noticed the initial suspicion of the tavern patrons about him had changed. He mentioned it to Darrca.

"Hera told them of your bravery against the Borrs," she replied. "Now, they expect you will track down Yartha. Another Gallaeci to hang from the closest tree."

"He won't get that lucky," Urith grunted as he followed her up to the second floor.

"I should make Hera my skald," he told her as they heard Dutra's footsteps following them.

When they reach the second floor, the open area held several straw beds. There were blankets pulled up around one area that appeared ready for the queen. She walked to one blanket and pulled it back. A small table next to the straw held a bowl. Urith watched as she took water from the bowl and splashed her face. He smiled when Darrca visibly shook from the bracing water. Then, the woman pulled down her robe to clean her neck. He turned from the display, which aroused him.

Even though the straw at the first bed he reached carried a stench, Urith didn't care. He carefully pulled off his tunic and chain mail. After he got off his padded undershirt, he told Dutra to bring over a burning lantern which hung near the stairs. The boy held the lamp for Urith to inspect his injured chest. The dark bluish-purple splotches from his broken ribs extend out from the center.

"Nothing I can do about this, but let it heal," Urith grimaced as he felt his muscles tensing. He looked over at Dutra.

"Alright, get your robe off so we can clean up your wound. Turun gave me some ground herbs to put on the area. From now on, you need to know how to clean and bind your wounds. After battle, there are never healers to help."

The boy set down the lamp and pulled off his robe. As he worked with Dutra, Urith felt someone watching them. He glanced over to see Darrca standing by her bed. Her stare caused him to miss a question from the boy. Then, Dutra noticed the Esterblud's focus.

He just smiled.

~~~
~~~

The sky turned to purple outside as dawn awoke. Mekan came out of a dream with a wave of fire from her leg that woke her. She found Hera dozing in a chair next to her. Numbness filled her backside and when the woman moved, another wave of pain filled her hip and thigh. Her grunt caused Hera to jerk awake.

"Now, don't be moving around," he warned as he came to her cot. "The leg has to mend, and you'll be on your back for a while."

Mekan looked down to see a series of wood shafts around her thigh, tied together with several loops of thin rope. Hera went over and brought a mug of water for her.

"Drink this down and I can tell you all about it."

She gulped down the drink, then her eyes widened.

"I'll need to find a latrine soon!"

The man smiled.

"We'll work it out when the time comes. Now, to the main point, Turun says you'll recover and walk again."

Mekan stared at him for a moment, then handed the mug back.

"Hera, you've always been a lousy liar. Tell me what she really said."

He dropped his head and turned away to place the cup on the nearby table. When he finally came back, he refused to look at her.

"The odds are you'll have a limp, maybe worse. Phillo shattered the bone so the mending will take longer, and it'll be more difficult. Turun is working on a better splint to help you. You'll stay here while the queen and I return to Cymeer."

Mekan sucked in her breath at the news.

"At least that calward is dead. What about Yartha?"

"It's alright, vengeance will come as Urith leaves to hunt him down this morning. I wish I could join him."

Mekan nodded as her eyes closed for a moment.

"You didn't want to kill him."

Her tone was soft.

"How dare you imply that?" the man lashed out.

"You look me in the eye and tell me the same story as last night," she looked at him. "I remember what you said about arriving in the town with the farmers. I also know you hung the Borrs in this town. Yartha didn't escape you."

Her eyes widened.

"You let him go. You want Urith to catch him."

His silence confirmed her thought.

"Hera, you know what that Borr did to me. Why leave it to the Esterblud?"

He remained silent before he glanced down. Mekan's perplexed expression pained him.

"Yartha travels to Esterblud. So will Urith."

"I see. You let cursed Borr escape because of your jealousy about Urith."

Her accusing tone caused Hera to come next to her bed. He kneeled by her.

"No, I would never stop you from having vengeance on Yartha. There's no way he'll survive. I broke his other arm and sent him away. He is the only bait for Urith. The Esterblud will kill him slowly and brutally for all the injuries. And Urith will go away from our land."

"You say it wasn't jealousy, then what was the reason?"

Hera glanced around the room, then lowered his voice.

"Queen Darrca," he told her. "Did you notice her attraction to him?"

Mekan looked puzzled.

"Do you think she'd make an Esterblud her lover? She's not that foolish. Besides, Urith cannot replace you as an advisor. No Rarfell tribe would follow him."

"No, I don't think Darrca will do such a thing. However, she's naïve enough to put herself in a position that will give her problems. They always opposed me about bringing foreign warriors into our land. Can you imagine what the king of Cahmais will do should he find out about an Esterblud working so closely with our queen? Besides, Lerah will use the Esterblud's presence to his advantage. With the help of the Borrs, he might split apart our lands. I know Darrca carries a need for revenge, which blinds her to the problems that any Esterblud help will bring to Rarfell."

"The queen talked about her plans for Urith after you left." Mekan closed her eyes. "She believes he'll follow her, no matter what happens. You were correct in getting him away." She paused, then looked over.

"Did you know he made promises to me? Urith might return. Especially if he knows you've done this."

"I can handle the Esterblud," Hera stated confidently. "He's large, but inexperienced in the ways of our world."

"I'm glad you think so. But I must ask why you're here with me? You are a noble, and I am not. I can give you little but my companionship, especially as a cripple."

Hera smiled, his eyes never leaving hers.

"I would think such things are obvious. You will find happiness with me. I have no ambition for a title and no law of Rarfell can stop me from bringing us before the priests and the gods."

"I've seen you look at me," she agreed. "But can you still care about a cripple the same way? You know that I've found other men to keep me happy. Even now, you should hate me."

Hera took her hand.

"As I hung in the palace, I decided about you. I told myself that should I live, nothing to keep us apart. It helped drive me with the same passion I have for getting our queen to rule again over our kingdom. Together, you and I can rebuild a world and keep the queen on the right path."

Mekan shut her eyes and squeezed his hand.

"Then you shall have a partner."

~~~

As the two lovers decided their paths, they heard an ossane galloping by. Urith followed the light of the early morning sun out of the village. His mount's breaths gave off a small wispy cloud as they rode along, and the bracing air smelled better than the musty smell of his bed.

He slowed the mount when he reached the edge of the village, where he found a bored man in a dirty Rarfell tunic. The man leaned on his halberd and nodded as Urith trotted by. Among the trees, he saw the handful of prisoners stripped of their belongs and tied to trees. The noise of crying, nearly naked children trying to stay warm in the embrace of their shivering mothers made him stare for a moment before he spurred his ossane down the road.

Your men who now hang from the tree across the road!

As the shadows of the forest road slowly overtook him, Urith tried to focus on his revenge. Still, he could not escape the images in his mind. The aftermath of battles always brought widows and orphans. It became something a warrior learned to dismiss or lock away. The cycle remained the same with the aftermath of battles or invasions. Starvation, rape, and slavery often fell upon those remaining alive on the losing side. While the wives and children were not responsible for the damage their men inflicted, they still suffered at the hands of the victors. While a few overlords
~~~

tried to control their warriors, many times, the victors did what they wanted while still covered in the blood of their enemies. The skalds seldom spoke about the captive's fortune when the victorious warriors overran a village. Slaughter of innocents was never heroic

Traveling along the path to Esterblud, Urith kept a sharp eye on the frost-covered dirt. The hoof prints he noticed didn't tell him much. Nothing stood out to show a lame animal. However, one set of prints wandered back and forth across the road like a drunken farmer returning from the tavern. The Esterblud smiled at the thought of a heathmead warming his body while he pushed on.

In the late afternoon, as he rounded a bend in the road, Urith's mount suddenly grew nervous. Bucking and whinnying, the animal forced the warrior to stop. While he patted his mount on the animal's neck, the warrior heard a snarling pack of *kuons* nearby. Normally, the ferocious creatures avoided human roads. It could only mean that one of their kills remained close.

Realizing the risk to his ossane, Urith slid off the saddle and tied the reins to a nearby tree. He pulled a spear that hung from the saddle before heading toward the noise. As he scouted the area, the warrior heard the snarls of the pack, then he heard the cry of a human. The man hurried toward the sound.

When he came out of a thin line of bluetrees, Urith found a small group of kuons ripping into a dead ossane's belly. With their massive pincer like teeth, the predators pulled out the bloody entrails to feast. Several paces away, the warrior spotted the rider still struggling to survive. Urith immediately recognized Yartha despite the blood covering his face. Unable to defend himself, the Borr rolled and kicked at the two kuons attacking him. As he ran over, Urith saw one predator rush toward Yartha's exposed abdomen while the other pulled on the screaming man's arm. The kuon's massive incisors cut deep into Yartha's lower belly. Swiftly, the second predator joined to disembowel the thrashing man.

Urith hurled the spear he carried, which struck a kuon in the hindquarter. As the creature yipped in pain, its partner turned, holding part of Yartha's intestines in its jaws. The kuon attacked Urith as he pulled his sword. Urith quickly killed the predator. The other kuon limped away with the spear still stuck in its back.

The Esterblud stood over Yartha. He recognized the man was beyond help. Urith glanced over at the kuons who continue to rip apart the ossane.

"Well, Esterblud, we've finally finished our path together. It's funny how the Fates robbed you of your glory." The Borr's mocking whisper reached him.

"What are you talking about? You're about to feed these kuons."

Yartha's smile was mostly a grimace as he shuddered.

"Hera sent you back to Esterblud and you're revenge on me means nothing. You're too dense to realize it. I was bait, you fool."

The dying man recognized the disbelief on Urith's face.

"Hera broke my good arm and put me on a lame ossane so I couldn't escape you. You notice where the road leads. We're only a couple of sunrises away from your home," he coughed up blood with a groan. When he finished, he smiled.

"I took everything you wanted. Now I have nothing to regret."

He saw Urith glancing at the pack of kuons who remained uninterested in him.

"One more thing to remember me. I had your woman on my terms," he taunted the Esterblud. "She wept and pleaded while I enjoyed her. I wanted you to know this. You can tell her I get the last laugh."

"Not likely," Urith growled as he swept his sword blade across the top of the ground.

Yartha's head tumbled away. The kuons looked up briefly before returning to their meal. Urith walked over to pick up his enemy's head. The eyes remained open, staring at him.

When Urith returned to his ossane, he debated his next steps. The Borr's words gnawed at him. Hera lied to him and sent him after Yartha. However, Urith didn't understand the reason. Perhaps it was Mekan. He saw the Rarfell leader keep a steady watch on the woman. Then again, Darrca's interest in Urith might influence Hera's decision. Either way, the devious nature of the plan infuriated the Esterblud.

Dishonorable cur!

The warrior planned on showing Mekan the head of Yartha, as promised. Then he vowed to confront Hera. In his mind, Urith had the right to a *fealth*, a one-on-one battle of honor with the Rarfell.

When Urith arrived back at the village, he entered the tavern to find Dutra waiting at the tavern for him.

"I knew you'd come back," he said.

"I guess you know me too well," Urith growled. "How is your shoulder?"

Dutra told him he was better.

"The queen ordered you to go to Eleb. She's heading there after picking up more fighters from villages along the way."

Is that the only thing she told you?

"Well, she appeared upset you left without warming her bed," he replied smugly.

"Another comment like that and I'll cuff you, then make you walk to Eleb." Urith scowled at him. "I take it Mekan is still here. Have you seen her?"

"Yes, she's doing better, but Hera told Darrca she'll probably be lame. He asked the queen to allow him to go to the priests. I think he wants Mekan to make vows with him."

"Yes, that's not a surprise. Go pack your ossane, then bring it and my mount to Turun's home." He ordered the young man. "Don't forget to get us food and drink." He pulled out his money bag and tossed it to the boy. "Don't spend all of it. There's armor in the corner there from the dead Borrs. Find a breastplate and helmet for yourself."

When Urith entered the healer's home, he saw the fear and annoyance in Mekan's eyes. Holding a bag in his hand, he stepped to her bed while dismissing the old woman. The Esterblud watched her leave before he turned to her.

"You seemed surprised to see me. Didn't you expect me to return with this?" He pulled out the head of Yartha out of the bag. The warrior tossed it on the ground. "I'll let you figure out what you want to do with it."

He turned to walk away.

"Urith, don't leave yet!"

The Esterblud stopped. He refused to look at her.

"Hera sent you after Yartha for the right reason. You should go back to your home."

"It's none of your concern," Urith told her.

"Don't confront Hera. You'll lose. I swear that he's protecting you."

The Esterblud glared at her.

"Yes, he should have told you the truth. But your presence with Queen Darrca will lead to disaster for everyone."

"I've seen your change about Hera as we've traveled. It's in your eyes. You've will say anything to protect him from a *fealth*, now."

Mekan tried to sit up and her moan caused Urith to turn back. She took a breath, waiting for the pain to subside.

"I've made my choice, but you're wrong. I wouldn't lie to you. We shared a couple of moments, nothing more. You never had a claim over me, you know that!" She watched him look away.

"Ask yourself why you want to stay with Darrca. She's grasping for anyone to help her take over Rarfell. She's not thinking about the elders of our tribes who resent outsiders. You endanger everything that we work for. Your vengeance is now complete. Return to your home."

Urith's hard stare barely softened.

"That's for Darrca to decide, not Hera."

Mekan carefully leaned back.

"Fine, I'm just a farmer's daughter. I listened to you and Rech speak about your arrival. You said that your brother considered him to be a wise man. Ask yourself if he would approve of you staying in Rarfell? Ask yourself what makes you stay here. Is it for your honor or your need for something else?"

The Esterblud walked to the door. He placed his hand on the wooden door handle and paused.

"That's my business, isn't it?"

Then, Urith left Mekan.

~~~
~~~

It was two afternoon's later when Urith and Duta reached Eleb. As they traveled, Urith remained quiet, barely speaking to his talkative shadow. Dutra remained unperturbed by the silence. When they arrive, they found trees filled with naked bodies, including women. They rode to the building, where a group of villagers milled around a long, narrow building. He guessed it was the hall of the village mear. Many towns in Kamin placed the central meeting building across the road from the tavern. The crowd went silent as the two riders come to a stop.

"I'm looking for Queen Darrca and Hera. Are they here?"

"What's an Esterblud wanting with our queen?" A big man wearing a leather apron and holding a mallet stood in Urith's path. Urith narrowed his eyes as two more joined the man. He placed his hand on his sword handle.

"Blacksmith, do you wish to find the underworld today? Anyone who wishes to die can stand in my way," Urith growled. His sneer smile caused the men to cast hesitant glances.

"Oh, clear out of here," the large warrior pushed through a small group.

Inside, he found Darrca sitting in a large chair in the middle of the room. The table on one side of her chair held a white-hair man who glared at Urith's interruption of his conversation. The man hurried over to stop the Esterblud.

"Leave here now!"

Urith ignored him and continued toward the queen. He noticed Darrca's eyes brighten as she watched the confrontation.

"By the gods, I'll have our villagers haul you away." The man continued.

"Now I'm worried," Urith sneered. "That crowd couldn't stop me from entering the building. Now sit down before I get upset!"

The Esterblud stopped in front of Darrca, who frowned. She wore a haphazard uniform of sorts with a long white tunic with purple embroidery, along with leather breeches. A leather belt encircled her waist, and she had a dagger sheathed in the belt.

"Urith, your presence is welcome, but your manner is not. This is Karw. He is a warrior and an elder of the Cyr tribe who just returned from Cahmais. He's brings me important news."

Urith glanced over at the man, who glared back.

"Darrca, my apologies for the intrusion. Yartha is dead and his head delivered to Mekan. Now I'm here to speak with Hera. We have much to discuss. I want to know why he sent me after a man he captured, then released."

The queen's expression changed to surprise, and then she pursed her lips.

"No doubt to send you back to your homeland. I believe Hera considers you a rogue who'll upset the delicate balance among those who fight for Rarfell. If that is all you have for me, return to the tavern and wait for when I want to see you."

Momentarily stunned by the dismissive order, Urith stood there. His eyes narrowed, but he remained quiet as he turned and left the room. The Esterblud pushed through the few people standing near the door. Still fuming, he crossed the street. He didn't see Dutra silently fall in behind him. They entered the nearly empty tavern.

Urith silently raged as he drank another mug of drink the locals called *wamper*. It had the slightly sweet taste of his favored heathmead, but the drink was weak as water. The Esterblud felt little effect from half a dozen mugs.

Dutra sat quietly next to the warrior on the bench near the back of the tavern. The boy watched every move of his mentor. He understood Urith's temper and remained silent despite the many questions he had.

From their vantage point, they watched the people entering the solemn room. Many of the families were already back at their homes, preparing for the next day of travel. Those in the building were single men who talked bravely about their upcoming journey to remove their enemy. A scowl crossed the Esterblud's face when a guard entered the tavern in a battered Rarfell tunic which was too long for his short stature. He wore a leather helmet and leather leggings. However, the older man with dark eyes had the massive arms of a tradesman or a blacksmith and he carried a wicked-looking sickle-sword with a hook-like end point. Urith recognized the unusual weapon as a *tutan*, difficult to wield effectively without experience.

The guard immediately came toward Urith.

"Queen Darrca states you may see her now. Come with me."

Slamming his mug down, Urith rose. He glanced back at the boy.

"Make sure you've sharpened the swords and spears by the time I'm back."

Urith followed his escort back to the hall. Outside, a small group of men in Rarfell tunics acted as the guards for the queen. As the two men entered the building, Urith looked over their weapons and listened to bits of their conversation. It did not impress him. The blacksmith noticed the disapproval.

"You don't think our men can fight?"

"I have my doubts that farmers who waited for warriors to set your village free." Urith growled. "Peasants are usually the first to run."

The guard stopped him by grabbing his chain mail.

"You're young and you judge people without knowledge. Some of us fought battles and killed men before you suckled your mother's tit. I led the life of a mercenary once. I picked up my weapons and killed Borrs when they took over. A noble who trains from youth and carries the best weapons and armor cannot know what a peasant must endure to keep his family fed."

He released Urith.

"I noticed how you treated my son when you arrived. It's true many of my people lack a uniform and some lack experience in battle. However, a farmer's sickle and a blacksmith's hammer will kill men. Only someone must organize and train those men properly. Otherwise, they are just peasants to be slaughtered. Hera knows this, as do people like me. You should ask questions and learn the answers before you open your mouth."

The Esterblud watched the man leaving. His initial anger changed as he remembered a similar encounter with his father. A grin came to his face.

"Blacksmith!" He called out.

The guard turned back.

"I deserved that! My father told me the same thing once. I guess I chose to forget it," Urith told him, then went into the room.

The Esterblud saw the queen hunched over an open scroll, intent on reading the contents from the light of a single candle that burned next to her. Other parchments lay on the table where she sat.

Darrca wore a white dress which was pinned by a brooch over one shoulder, along with golden trim and a red cloth belt tied around her waist. She heard Urith approaching and glanced over. She returned to her work.

"As you've requested, I'm here." He announced, crossing his arms as he stopped.

A frown appeared on her face as she stood.

"You remain upset at my dismissal. Yet, you gave me no other choice. I'm queen of Rarfell."

Urith nodded, then he glanced back at the entrance to the room.

"I was just reminded of that," he told her.

"I can't have you barging into a room with people whose support I need." She picked up a scroll. "Karw brought these parchments which outline the offer of help from King Asgurd of Cahmais. I realize he's a hated enemy of your people. However, Karw thinks I should consider Asgurd's proposal."

The Esterblud's eyes momentarily widen at the news, then his expression turned dark.

"I've warned you about King Penhda's reaction to Rarfell falling under Asgurd's influence."

"And I must act like a virgin bride trying to decide between my suitors." She placed the parchment back on the table, then walked around the table toward him. "If your diplomat brother, Pehnuwick, advised me, no doubt he would suggest such a strategy. Isn't that really what's best for my land?"

Caught off-guard by her suggestion, Urith dropped his arms. He swept his hand through his long hair while he considered Pehnuwick's insightful advice over the seasons.

"Aye, my brother would approve. You must do what's best for your people." He finally agreed.

Darrca came by his side and curled her arm around his as she led Urith to the table.

"I'm glad you agree. In fairness, I'm just learning how much I don't know about ruling in this world of warriors," the queen confessed. Her expression darkened.

"However, I know that I'm strong enough to take on any man now! I changed from the girl you first met."

Darrca waved her hand over the papers on the table. "This is only a small part of what I must learn to become an effective ruler of my land. I must also develop skills to consider the motives and reasons behind the words of those who advise me."

Urith looked over at the woman holding his arm.

"Your insight does you credit" he sighed when he thought back to what the guard told him earlier.

"Maybe it's easier for a warrior to act like a bully. We find the training to crack a skull more agreeable than understanding the reasons behind the reasons we fight."

She patted him on the arm.

"Well, warriors bring the downfall of bandits and that's something that I need. You already have my eternal gratitude for your actions against Phillo and Yartha. Yet I have other plans for you if you're interested."

The queen led him into the darkness toward the back of the hall. He saw the sliver of light coming from the curtain over a door.

"I wish for you to stay with me, Urith. I want you to lead a new Cymeer Company that I'm building." Darrca stopped, then untied the red belt around her waist.

"Add my colors to your tunic and I'll give you fighters to finish off my enemies."

"I'm not sure," Urith glanced around the dark room. He breathed in her scent. "I'm an Esterblud. Your people consider me nearly as bad as the Borrs."

"You will not act as an Esterblud. As I recall, you volunteered to help our cause. I'm asking that you keep my enemies from reinforcing while my people gather their strength. Let me handle my people."

She pointed to the table.

"It just so happens I read the works of Heptarc and I will follow his strategy. I want the guards you lead to drive out the Borrs along the Esterblud border. You will remember what they did to us and hang the men from the closest tree. When you're not fighting, I want you to build a militia force at each village so no enemy can enter our lands undetected again."

He stopped the queen, turning to her.

"This is a great honor. But I must ask if you've spoken with others about this?"

Darrca expression darkened.

"Have you not heard what I've told you earlier? I'm the ruler of Rarfell."

The big warrior nodded.

"As you explained, you must know the reason behind the advice given to you. However, a ruler cannot spring a plan upon your people without knowledge of the cost to your position."

His careful reply caused her to smile.

"Urith, I'm not a fool. I understand Hera believes that your continued presence will cause problems for me within Rarfell. That's the reason you will travel to the lands by Esterblud and remove that green tunic. It will calm the concerns of my advisers. Hera will build the army to overrun Cymeer. He carries a natural ability to that task."

She saw his face darken at the name.

"Hera believes that he's protecting Rarfell. I have confidence in his ability and trust in his judgement. I'm asking that you accept the same risk that I'm willing to accept."

The Esterblud stared at her for a moment. Their eyes locked and finally, he grinned.

"You've been planning this for a while."

She nodded.

"I understand an Esterblud won't accept payment for a life. This is a step for me to make things right between us."

"Well, I've taken koinons for my sword. Some say that's what brought me to Rarfell."

The queen laughed and took him by the elbow to the curtain and pulled it back. The small room held a bed with a table holding a candle.

"I won't offer koinons." She reached up and kissed his cheek. Darrca smiled at his embarrassment.

"You told me once that you've had a wife. I don't think you should find embarrassment in touch." Her surprised expression at his reaction made him smile.

"No, I don't. Instead, I'm trying to remember my place." He explained.

Darrca took his hand and used it to pull off the brooch. Her robe flopped open, exposing her breasts. The woman brought his rough hand to one breast. He lightly squeezed, and she reacted with a quick inhale. Urith leaned close and kissed her on the lips.

"Don't remember your place for the moment," the queen breathed heavily. "Remove that cold chain mail so we can experience the warmth of our bodies together."

"This might not last between us," he warned. "Many times, the world doesn't allow what we might want."

Darrca nodded in agreement, pulling the curtain shut.

"True, but we can have this night, which is only ours." Her eyes searched his. "Something we can always share, even when apart."

He lifted the woman from the ground as her robe fell away. She put her arms around his neck as Urith stepped over to the bed.

Chapter 9: A Broken Land

The height of the growing season was in the air as the eastern wind warmed the highlands. In the many sunrises since he left Queen Darrca, Urith and his diverse group of fighters established a bloody reputation in their hunt for the Borrs. The Cymeer Company fought ruthlessly, their focus on the holdouts that once followed their dead leader, Phillo. Blood and gore stained the blue tunics of the mercenaries from their deadly battles as they scattered their enemies, hiding in the remote valleys of dense forests. As leader of the group, Urith tried to hide his Esterblud warrior status by wearing the brown robe of a farmer. However, the red belt given by Queen Darrca hung from his baudrik belt as a symbol of their mission.

Now close to the border of Esterblud, the group rode for the last village in Rarfell, which fell during the invasion of the Borrs. Some holdouts trying to escape into the mountainous backcountry of Rarfell met in battle with Urith and his small group of Cymeer mercenaries that morning. Pushing their ossanes hard, the members of the Cymeer Company sought to cutoff any Borrs who might flee into the backcountry of Esterblud.

Just as the sun was sitting in the East, Urith saw the small hamlet of Marala ahead. The village sat along a narrow stream that carried water from the mountains in the distance. Galloping past the empty ossane trader's stables, Urith sent a couple of fighters on a side trail. Other fighters rode on to secure other buildings of the hamlet while the Esterblud pulled to a stop in front of the tavern. His shadow, Dutra, pulled alongside him and automatically took the reins.

"Stay close, we don't know what to expect here," Urith glanced over at the young boy, then focused his attention on the nearby trees which held no hanging body. The Esterblud turned to Prita, a Ynyover fighter who became an indispensable second leader to Urith during their time together.

"Prita, you come with me. We'll see who lives here."

The massive man nodded and slid off his ossane. His chain mail scraped across the large blue-colored shield he carried on the side of his mount.

Prita joined Urith at the entrance to the building while carrying his decorated *bardar*. The elongated battle axe head was perfect for knocking through thick wooden doors. However, there was no need to use the weapon, since a purple-robed woman opened the door.

"What band of mercenaries are you?" Her scathing tone offered no hint of fear from the large men in front of her.

"We're commissioned by Queen Darrca to take care of the scum Borrs," Urith told her as he pushed his way inside. A single bed sat in one corner while a table backed to a bench near the wall. A tall man sitting at the table avoided Urith's gaze. The simple accommodations revealed nothing to him. However, the nervous man caught his attention. He stepped closer and focused his questions on the man.

"A band of men wearing the face tattoos of these scum came through two sunrises ago. Which path did they take away from here?"

"To…to the north," he stammered out.

"How many?" Urith placed his hand on his sword.

The man glanced over at the woman.

"There were five men," the old woman interrupted as she stepped next to the table. "I'm Wrren, the village mear. The Borrs left this area."

"That's strange, your accent is not Cyer, nor Esterblud." Urith glanced back at Prita, whose dark eyes narrowed at the news. "My friend beheaded a Borr this morning. Before the man died, he claimed that the people of Marala were dead. The prisoner smiled as he recounted how they treated the villagers here."

He heard Dutra come into the room.

"They found the graves," the boy calmly told him.

He remained as Urith nodded, then slid out his Clovel Sword.

"You should know about the Cymeer Company," Urith looked at the woman in the purple robe, his gray eyes revealing the death he dealt out over the past days of fighting with the Borrs.

"The Borr women become widows before we sell them to the slavers of Cahmais."

The woman backed to the table as her bluster temporarily drained away.

"The man next to you tries to hide the tattoos on his neck with the hood of his robe. Besides, our prisoner told us the mear of this village was the first to die when they arrived."

Suddenly, the nervous man pushed the table toward Urith. The edge caught him in the leg, sending him back. As the Borr tried to escape through a side door, he wasn't fast enough. Prita struck the bandit in the back with his battleaxe. The force of the blow sent the man through the door. Only able to use his hands to crawl, the Borr quickly died from the next blow swung by the Ynyover fighter. The old woman cried out, trying to stop the man's death, but Urith pushed her to the ground in disgust.

"There's no disguise to save you, foul wench. I suspect the Borr who told us about the massacre of Marala was one of your children. The Borrs killed every man after raping their women and children in front of them. We'll let the queen decide your fate for the massacre of this village."

His ominous tone didn't faze the woman who now stared at him.

"You killed my sons, you scarred spawn of Caruun. I curse you!"

Urith gave her his scarred smirk.

"Save your strength, woman. You're going to need it for your journey. Soon, you'll meet your worthless sons in the underworld."

~~~

Two mornings later, the mercenaries rode the narrow road heading back to Cymeer. The few women prisoners and their children who remained in the village followed, riding behind them. Two of the men of the Cymeer Company had a young woman sitting behind them as they wound their way through the valley. The Borr women were now the spoils of war for the warriors. While the tribes of Esterblud took no slaves, the mercenaries of his group came from other areas of Kamin who had no such rules or tradition. Urith's experience with the Borrs left him with little sympathy for the plight of those they captured.

Dutra remained on one side of Urith while Prita rode on the other side. The Ynyover warrior whistled the same tune since they had first rode together. The Esterblud believed it was the only tune the man knew.

"Prita told me that we're less than a day's ride from Esterblud. Do you miss your homeland?" Dutra's question brought Urith out of his thoughts.

"Yes, I suppose so," the warrior admitted. "We're close to completing our charge from the queen. I'm sure I'll return soon."
~~~

He glanced over to see Dutra considering the answer. He smiled to himself.

Near a bend in the road, Urith noticed a blue clad rider wearing a leather helmet galloping toward them. To his surprise, a skinny young woman came to a stop in front of him. She carried only a dagger for protection, but her confident manner told him she feared little.

"I'm looking for the Cymeer Company," the messenger announced.

"That is who you've found," the warrior grunted. "What words do you bring for us?"

She glanced at the men who gathered around her.

"I'm spreading the word of Queen Darrca's victory. Rarfell's army has taken Cymeer."

There was a cheer that rose from the men, and the girl smiled. When several of the fighters asked for details, the messenger shook her head.

"That's all I know for the moment. Karw sent me to find the Esterblud called Urith."

"That's me," he replied.

"The queen orders that you return with me."

"It will be a slow journey," Urith snorted. "I have prisoners who can't keep up with the speed of your ossane."

The messenger looked over at the line of prisoners and frowned.

"The queen insisted you should come with me. The rest of the company can follow with these prisoners," she suggested.

"Alright," Urith nodded, then turned to Prita.

"You heard the queen's instructions. I'll ride ahead. You keep the men in line. We'll drink to our success in Cymeer."

The hulking man pulled his ossane close to Urith's.

"Don't forget that you buy the first round for the men. These prisoners should bring us enough koinons to enjoy our time there," Prita grinned.

Spurring his mount, Urith and the messenger rode ahead. Then, the Esterblud realized Dutra galloped right behind them. Glancing back at Dutra, Urith grinned.

"I keep forgetting that I have a shadow," he informed the messenger.

~~~

"I don't like it. He should know the truth," Darrca stated as she paced the floor. "I sent him to remove our enemy. Urith's done that."

"And more! His reputation is spreading. Soon, the fact that an Esterblud leads the Cymeer Company will reach King Asgurd. It's something that you must stop." The large man calmly stated as he watched the woman.

The queen turned to him.

"I would think you should enjoy the idea of a Cahmais king upset with a Rarfell queen."

His gray eyes twinkled with delight, and she noticed that his broad face carried a similar smile.

"Oh, the irony is interesting to me. However, the time comes for you to make this hard decision. The problem for you will turn into a problem for my people and my king if you don't act."

Darrca took a seat on the newly built throne. She glanced at Hera, then Karw.

"Do you agree with our visitor's view of the situation?"

Karw quickly nodded.

"I wasn't happy with the idea of a band of mercenaries traveling around our lands. However, your decision to use them was a wise one. The Cymeer Company's efforts to remove the Borrs allowed our men and women to
~~~

concentrate on building an army to take our capital back. I suspect you always envisioned that the mercenary's work was temporary. Since we have no need for the company now, I believe we should disband them."

"I take it you agree as well, Hera." Darrca placed her hand over her mouth as a wave of nausea struck her. The visitor noticed her complexion pale slightly during the reaction.

"Yes, I believe it's time for the company to disperse. Our Rarfell army is still inexperienced and unruly, but we can handle the remaining bandits."

"Perhaps I find your confidence misplaced. I hear that our new warriors take out their petty disputes against their neighbors." Darrca replied as she stood again.

"I expect my advisors to give me the complete truth. Now, is my information incorrect?"

Hera frowned.

"No, I've seen such things. However, it is something we can handle. We need to send these mercenaries home. The skalds are already spreading tales of their deeds."

"It is in your best interests that my overlord seeks for you to disband this group. It brings fighters with loyalties that might undermine your rule," the visitor leaned forward.

Darrca gave the man a grin.

"I'm sure your king thinks only of my welfare. I'm sure he's not concerned with reports of volunteers coming from tribes along our border."

The visitor returned the grin.

"I'm not here to insult the queen's intelligence. However, I'm sure that your use of, let us call them volunteers, to help you rebuild your defenses against our common enemy is something we can agree upon. In fact, my overlord will provide additional help should you agree to the idea."

Darrca observed him. She recognized the man's knowledge of her needs left her with a weak hand. Accepting his offer tilted her people into an alliance which might prove deadly to her rule.

"I think your offer is generous, but we are a proud people more suited to doing things on our own." Her tone remained sweet but firm. "Therefore, I've heeded my advisor's beliefs. I disbanded the company. Further, the Esterblud must leave." She looked out of the dingy window of her temporary home. The queen glanced back at the stranger.

"Never to return!"

The man nodded. His knowing expression bothered her, and she returned to staring out the window.

"You make a wise choice. Your people need to recover from the turmoil. Should another king decide to send volunteers to Rarfell…well, the future becomes difficult for everyone."

~~~

The smell of the burning wood struck Urith as he rode the now familiar road into Cymeer. At the top of the ridge, he saw the reason. Smoldering buildings inside the city still sent up black smoke to carry in the light wind. The trio of riders passed the gates, where two guards milled around, looking bored.

Urith found Karw in front of the barracks, which remained untouched in the fighting. He stood in a group of men and women who were mostly armed and wore various tunics and robes of their trades. As the queen predicted, Hera's ragtag army succeeded in overtaking Cymeer. Urith watched as Dutra guided his ossane closer to the nearby
~~~

bodies of a few Borrs who lay where they died. After a quick look, the young man rode back to join his mentor.

Urith and Dutra waited on their mounts while the messenger went to Karw. The queens' advisor looked over at the Esterblud, then whispered something to the man closest to him.

"Our esteemed mercenary returns." Karw came closer with a broad smile. The warrior slid off the saddle as the Rarfell fighters gathered around the two men.

"The men of the Cymeer company are bringing the last prisoners we've found. I believe all the villages are now controlled by your people. The Borrs flee your lands."

"You've done well. As you can see, the queen has retaken her capital. She now enjoys the delight of watching the Borrs die slowly in the pen they constructed. Soon, the rebuilding will start."

Urith looked over at the remains of the buildings destroyed during the fighting.

"You have a lot of work to do."

"Yes, no doubt it will take time," Karw agreed. He nodded to his men while the Esterblud looked away.

"First on the list will remove those who shouldn't be in Rarfell."

"Urith, look out!" Dutra called out.

The Esterblud couldn't avoid the two men who tackled him. After a brief struggle, a large Rarfell woman joined her comrades using a club to strike Urith in the head. Amid the laughter and hoots of the crowd, the men dragged the stunned Urith toward the barracks. Dutra tried to intervene, but one man in the crowd pulled him from the saddle. The man carried the screaming boy into the building while the messenger gathered the two ossanes.

His wrists bound tightly behind him, Urith slowly came out of his groggy haze while the guards hauled him into a room. They placed him on a bench. Despite swirling in his head, the warrior noticed a silent Darrca standing by an open window. The wretched cries of someone outside caught his attention.

"Bring him over!" she ordered.

The Rarfell men pulled their prisoner to the window. Urith saw the horuks attacking and killing a Borr prisoner. He noticed another man in the cage next to the pen. As he watched, the guards left the room.

"Have you already disposed of your brother, Lerah?"

"No, he and the rest of Phillo's advisors escaped. Hera has scouts looking for them. Soon, he'll track them down."

"Yes, just like he helped me with Yartha," Urith replied.

Darrca ignored the comment.

"You witness what Phillo forced me to watch that day before he took me," she told Urith. He noticed the callousness in the queen's expression during the savage display. "It is a display meant to show power." She looked at him and gave a brief smile.

"You see, I've learned something from his brutality."

"Is that all you've learned?" He asked with a smirk.

"No, I've also found that I must give up certain things in order to be a queen."

"Should I reply with my sympathy?" His sarcasm brought the woman out of her memories.

"Like those horuks outside, Urith, you are an efficient and effective hunter of men. You and your men are already developing a reputation which I cannot have. It threatens my rule. The mercenaries will no longer fight for my cause." She turned to him. Darrca stepped closer, noticing her red cloth knotted around his baudrik belt which hung over his shoulder. She smiled at the memory.

"You've honored me by wearing this."

"I'm not sure about my choice," he growled. "You have a strange way of showing me things like honor and gratitude."

"You and I share a memory, not a future." Her manner turned cold, and she turned away. As she walked to the door, Queen Darrca absently rubbed her belly. She stopped and glanced back at the large warrior.

"I remember the words you told me on that night. You said that the world won't allow what we might want. Maybe you should consider yourself a prophet, since what you said is true. I'm sorry for the hate that will fill your heart. But I must do what's best for my future rule. Soon, you'll learn about the choice I made."

After the woman left, Hera entered the room along with several of his comrades.

"I see your plans coming from the queen. Are you here to enjoy the show? I assume I'm to join the Borrs in the cage below."

Hera walked over to the window at the sound of a terrified yell. He saw a horuk slashing into the unfortunate prisoner inside the pen.

"It's a thought, but you're too famous for such a death. Besides, I still respect the man who saved my life."

He turned back to the Esterblud, nodding to the guards on either side of the prisoner. They led Urith through the doors.

"I heard you wanted a fealth, so I went to the queen to let you have the honor of us dueling to the death."

"It won't be an honor for you. I've discovered that I enjoy killing since I've come to Rarfell," Urith growled as they reached the stone stairs.

"Well, you'll never get the chance. She turned me down."

"Why?" Urith glanced back.

Hera shrugged as he placed his hand on the warrior's shoulder.

"Maybe she didn't want me dead," he told him. "Or maybe she didn't want you dead."

The Rarfell leader pushed the captive down the stairs. Urith slammed into the steps hard, his head struck the rock wall as he tumbled down. He landed at the bottom in a heap. The Esterblud felt blood coming from his nose as he shook his head from the dizziness.

Hands lifted him to his feet, but Urith nearly collapsed again. The guards dragged him along the passageway to the main entrance. Urith's mount waited along with Dutra, who held the reins. The guards pushed the groaning warrior on his mount.

"Your treatment reinforces that fact that Karw just announced that you've been banished from Rarfell by the queen's order. You can't return."

"Now, you have no reason to worry about those who rode with you in the Cymeer Company. We welcome them to stay and help us rebuild as individuals. They did their job well, but we can't have mercenaries bring two king's rivalry into our land."

Urith looked down at Hera.

"You will return to Esterblud," the Rarfell leader stated. "Good luck to you."

He looked over at Dutra.

"Lead him to the crossroads!"

Hera slapped the rump of the Esterblud's ossane and the animal hurried away. He watched the two mounts take the road toward the gate, where a crowd gathered by Karw waited. Then Hera walked back into the barracks.

Dutra avoided the first object hurled in their direction as the two riders tried to leave Cymeer. Urith wasn't as fortunate as he could only duck with his arms still locked together behind him. Rotten food and trash hurled by the booing and hissing crowd caused the ossanes to speed up, nearly sending the Esterblud to the ground. Hanging on to the other mount's reins, Dutra directed his spooked animal toward the open gate. Soon, the riders past the guards hooting and laughing at the public humiliation.

Close to the walled city, Dutra brought the animals to a stop. He pulled his small dagger and cut the cord binding Urith's wrists. As the warrior rubbed the numbness away from his hands, he kept looking back at the town walls.

"You're lucky they let you leave alive," the boy told his mentor.

Urith nodded absently, then shook his head.

"No, they let me go with a warning."

"Why would they do this?" The young man raised his eyebrow at the idea.

"That's a good question. Maybe we'll find out when we reach the crossroads," the Esterblud looked back at the stiff blanket roll. He untied the roll and found his Clovel Sword and scabbard inside. To his surprise, a new red cloth belt wrapped around the scabbard. He hooked the sword scabbard into his belt. The warrior left the red cloth attached. He glanced over at Dutra.

"Not one word out of you!" Urith said while he tied his bedroll back behind the saddle. Then, he spurred his ossane away from Cymeer.

The two riders came upon the empty crossroads leading to Esterblud. Urith slowed his ossane while his shadow looked around. Soon, Urith noticed a familiar figure emerged from the trees on a white ossane.

As the stranger approached, Dutra stopped his mount with Urith. The young man kept glancing back and forth between the similar-looking men. The man coming toward them dressed in the green tunic of an Esterblud. He even had a black helmet like Urith that clanked against the side of the saddle.

"They did a good job on you, brother." Pehnuwick brought his ossane to a stop.

"Probably your cursed idea," the warrior growled ominously.

A frown crossed his brother's face.

"No! I'm offended that you would think so. Can you figure out why I'm here?"

"Aye, another of your trips to keep King Penhda happy. The question is why you didn't come to me first?" Urith wiped the drying blood from his upper lip with his sleeve.

"What makes you think I didn't? Searching the mountainous stretches between Cymeer and the Esterblud border takes valuable time. I knew you would return once the queen summoned you. You have a weakness for fair maidens. I recall an enslaved noble you brought back from Regiussa."

"Don't bring up things that are none of your affair," Urith grunted, then spit red saliva on the ground.

"Our overlord heard of your involvement here. Did you really think that wearing a brown robe would hide your identity? The colors of King Penhda's kinship guard cannot lead us into a war. Even worse, the rumors about Queen Darrca's closeness to you can only bring disaster to her. I thought you would recognize the danger." Pehnuwick pulled the reins to turn his ossane.

"I knew of the risk and so did she."

Urith's brother looked back.

"Alright, you knew and yet you let everyone know an Esterblud led a group of mercenaries in a land close to King Asgurd. Come, we can talk about your lack of judgement on the way out of this land."

"What makes you think I'll follow, brother? You're the one who lives to do as the king and his people bid."

His brother glared at him.

"Because our king demands that you return. I'm only here to calm things and let the queen play at ruling an insignificant kingdom. While you've been taking women and children as prisoners, other events threaten our lands from the North. You should enjoy the coming battle!"

Pehnuwick spurred his ossane toward Esterblud. Urith watched him for a moment as Dutra waited.

"You heard him," Urith growled. "If you're staying with me, you'll get to see my homeland."

The warrior followed his brother as a grinning Dutra joined him.

~~~

When the Esterbluds and Urith's young protégé reached the border of Rarfell, on the other side of the small country, a small group of men and women entered the lands of Cahmais. In the column's front was Sarcam, who rode next to Aralla. Lerah followed closely behind them, along with the few remaining Gallaeci warriors of Phillo, who escaped the city of Cymeer. Behind them were the wives of Phillo in a wagon
~~~

pulled by erbas. The few slaves they still had jogged along to keep up.

Aralla and Sarcam drove the group hard, intent on reaching the village of Spural before nightfall. The village was a known spot for Gallaeci traders and their families to rest with their wagons before they moved west into the interior of Cahmais.

"I know you want to join your people when we reach Spural," Lerah stated, as he tried again to convince the men of his idea. "However, King Asgurd will provide us with koinons to return to Rarfell with our choice of fighters. I insist I should meet with Asgurd. He'll never let my sister remain as queen if he knows that I'm sympathetic to his cause."

"You're only sympathetic to your cause," scoffed Aralla. "He'll see you for what you are."

Lerah went silent, then took a different approach.

"Maybe so, but like you told me, I still have a use as the heir to the throne. Should my dear sister die, who better to help the Borrs re-establish their dream outside the eyes of King Asgurd?" He pushed his ossane closer to Aralla.

"All I'm asking Asgurd for is koinons to pay the people needed to remove Darrca. I certainly don't want him bringing his Aberffraw warriors into the lands. With the right people, I can return to Rarfell as the only option to be king when my sister dies."

The Borr glanced over with skepticism filling his face.

"And how do you remove the queen? You have no one to follow you. We've lost too many fighters to return." Aralla shook his head. "We can rebuild here."

Lerah looked over at the silent Sarcam.

"You know Asgurd remains suspicious of the Gallaeci and the Aberffraw will never allow your people to rise. How soon will it take before the king realizes the followers of

Facarm are in his land? Do you really believe that some Gallaeci trader won't take koinons for your location?"

Sarcam's glance over to Aralla was caught by Lerah. He pressed.

"Listen, you're both smarter than Phillo. That's why you survived. I've learned from watching you and your methods. I know you think that I'm weak. However, I have brains and a plan. Both of you can benefit. You want a movement to succeed. My ambition is to have the land that's rightfully mine."

"Why do you need Asgurd then?" Sarcam asked.

"I need him simply for the koinons to get a group who'll help me remove Darrca." Lerah smiled at the mental image of his dying sister.

"Be clear," Aralla warned.

"It's simple enough. There's only one group on Kamin that all rulers fear." Lerah replied with growing confidence.

"You mean death creepers!" Sarcam stated.

"Of course, who else but *fealharan* would do my bidding on the behalf of King Asgurd? For a bit of money, the king of Cahmais gets a loyal servant and my Gallaeci friends have a place to build their following unobserved."

The two Borrs glanced at the man riding between them.

"Perhaps you misjudged me?" Lerah smiled.

"Perhaps, then again, if you betray us, you'll wish that the fealharan are the one's killing you." Sarcam stated.

About the Author

Gordon Brewer is the pseudonym for a professional geek, history buff, and full-time dad who took up a challenge from his son to finish his first novel and enter the world of writing. Raised on a farm in Kansas, the author spent nearly five years in the US Navy traveling to 12 different countries during this time. After his discharge, he received his BS degree with majors in History and Political Science.

Over the next twenty years, Gordon focused on the business and IT world. His experiences left him with a need to explore wide-ranging interests in multiple genres, each with historical consideration given to the characters and settings.

Residing in Tennessee, he often uses his family and friends as unfortunate guinea pigs, forced to listen to his tales, no matter how poorly conceived they may be.

You can find out more about the author and upcoming books along with his other works at www.gordonbrewer.com.